The
Wildewood Chronicles
The Novellas Collection
1-3

Knight's Quest

B.A. Morton

Twisted Ink Publishing

The
Wildewood Chronicles
The Novellas Collection
1-3
Knight's Quest

© B.A. Morton 2015

Includes

Bad Blood

Assassin's Curse

The Burning Boy

For Kighe

A knight in the making

Strong, brave and true

Bad Blood

Novella One

The Crusader stronghold of Acre: 1272 A.D.

Miles of Wildewood discovers the boy, Edmund, at the mercy of his sworn enemy, Guy-de-Marchant. The feud between the two men has dark roots in an incident shrouded in secrecy and protected by a Templar oath. The boy's plight provides the catalyst for an escalation of hostilities. As a trial by combat is hastily arranged to settle the dispute, Miles' benefactor Hugh-de-Reynard seeks a favour from the future king and the Templars prepare for the inevitable backlash.

Miles must save the boy, but at what cost?

One

The heaving mass of militia blocked the narrow streets. Giant war-horses, fresh from battle and lathered white with sweat, wore the spattered blood of man and fellow beast like macabre trophies. Each animal fought the bit, shaking their massive heads and pawing the ground as they wrestled for control. The soldiers, fuelled with the adrenalin of the kill, paid little heed to the unfortunates trampled underfoot and pressed their chargers on regardless. All around, amid the din and chaos, Venetian traders tried in vain to save their wares as ramshackle stalls collapsed beneath the weight of horse and man. Servants laden with goods, mothers with infants clutched to their breast, the helpless and hopeless all desperately scrambled to safety as the armoured riders' laughter mocked their plight. Chivalry and honour had fallen victim to blood lust and the merchants of Acre howled their protest.

Miles of Wildewood confronted the scene with a mixture of anticipation and dismay. He'd not expected to come upon Guy-de-Marchant while the memory of Lincoln still pulsed like an angry wound. After journeying to The Holy Land at Prince Edward's decree and surviving twelve months of battle, and arduous conditions, it was ironic that Miles should come face to face with his enemy in a bustling market place in Acre.

Guy had swept into camp some weeks before with his entourage, a motley band of mercenaries and sycophants. Each man, a knight in name only, honour and chivalry defiled as they whiled away their evenings in drunken debauchery. By day, their viciousness on the battlefield had earned them a measure of respect from those who made killing their business. Miles suspected that Edward turned a blind eye to Guy's irreverent behaviour, as when all was said and done, the black-hearted son of a wealthy baron did achieve results, and for a prince barely one step away from the throne, victory by any means was essential.

Built upon fear and unwarranted cruelty, Guy's reputation, had been growing exponentially, and yet, Miles knew Guy for the coward beneath the veneer and that knowledge placed him in a dangerous position. He'd expected Guy to ensure his silence with a sword in his belly or a blade at his throat, after all, the wrong word in the right ear could seriously compromise Guy's campaign to curry the monarch's favour. Yet weeks had passed since his arrival and the two men, whether by design or happenstance, had barely crossed each other's path. Something was afoot and Guy was at the centre of it, Miles was convinced of that.

Now, despite Hugh-de-Reynard's orders to maintain a prudent distance, he could not avoid the man. In fact, his benefactor was most insistent that he put as much distance as possible between him and the man who could see him hanged. It was wise counsel, from one who was well aware of Miles' propensity for reckless acts. It would not do for the Templars' closely guarded secret to be put at risk by a hot-blooded act of revenge.

Miles reined in his own horse and raised a hand for his men to hold fast behind him.

"Miles..." Thomas Blackmore's urgent tone was accompanied by a gloved hand on his arm.

"The man is overdue a lesson in manners," replied Miles with a tight smile.

"You waste your breath and risk even more by engaging with him. Come away, before you do something you will live to regret."

"My only regret is not finishing this two years since."

"Remember Hugh's words..."

Miles shrugged away his companion's concern. "Hugh is elsewhere and this matter is long overdue. I shall attend to it now if Guy has the stomach for it."

Guy-de-Marchant emerged from the centre of the unruly rabble, his men forcing their horses aside to allow him passage through the melee. His mount had borne witness to the worst of the slaughter. Its mane was stiff with enemy blood. Astride the beast, Guy too was marked with the rancid entrails of war. He halted the horse, and behind, his men fanned out threateningly. Lifting his visor he threw a sly smile at the Templars before focusing his attention on Miles.

"Who do we have here, the Northumbrian upstart who believes himself a knight? You're a little late to the skirmish, Miles. The spoils are mine. There is naught left on the battlefield but bloody corpses."

The man had merely to open his mouth for Miles' stomach to churn with darkness and revenge. "I wager there is room for one more corpse if you'd care to accompany me out to Baybars' lair," he hissed in response.

"You speak of your own demise, Miles. You are not man enough to meet me in combat. You have Reynard to fight your battles with his silver tongue, and his Templars to watch your back. When will you cast aside your nursemaids and fight like the bastard you are?"

"Miles...," Thomas' low growl, cautioned once again, but heedless to the warning, Miles urged his horse forward until he and Guy were parallel, armoured plates clanking together as the horses jostled each other.

Standing tall in the stirrups he leaned into Guy, forcing the man to yield. The stench of death was overpowering. It hung about him like shroud. It took all of Miles' willpower not to recoil. "Brave words from a man with a small army at his beck and call, I wonder, would you be so fearless without them?"

Guy laughed unpleasantly. His men sidled closer. "You flatter yourself, Miles. You are naught but a peasant with dreams of grandeur. I have no need of men at arms to defeat you."

"Then this matter will be easily rectified. Draw your sword and we'll have done with it here and now."

"A common brawl in the market place, now why does that not surprise me?" Guy's lip curled into an ugly sneer. "Dear me, what will your saviour *The Fox* say about your uncivilised behaviour?" He yanked at the reins and an accompanying vicious kick sent his horse rearing angrily. Miles ducked to avoid the flailing hooves. There was not room to draw a weapon and he accepted reluctantly that on this occasion Guy was correct, it was neither the time nor place for a brawl. He gathered in the reins of self-control and eased his own horse out of the way.

"This is not over." He threw the words at Guy's retreating back and the man turned in the saddle and spat his contempt.

"Was that wise?" muttered Thomas as the riders bullied their way past, hurling curses and obscenities at the curious onlookers.

Exhaling his frustration Miles watched them go, torn between following and seeing an end to the issue once and for all, or accepting the sense of Thomas' counsel. Thomas was right. It was not wise to rattle the cage of such a man, a man who was privy to foul deeds, but he had to admit, it felt good to poke a stick at such a devil.

"Time will tell, Thomas," he answered evenly. "At present the roach is protected by the stone under which he scuttles. To ensure good triumphs over evil we must leave no stone unturned."

"We?"

Miles shot him a glance, "Are we not one against our enemies?"

"We are indeed, Miles, which is why we accept each other's advice and do not act alone. Hugh is at pains to protect you from yourself. I fear he has an arduous task."

Miles shrugged away Thomas' concern. "I'm no fool, Thomas. I recall the oath. I did not take it lightly. I know the importance of the secrets we keep. I would guard them with my life, as I would guard all of you, my comrades."

"Then do not risk what you hold so dear, Miles. There will be time aplenty for righting Guy's wrongs."

Miles nodded. The market place was not the ideal location to exact a fitting punishment on Guy. Overrun as it was with a populous whose loyalties were traded on a daily basis. Who knew the allegiance of those who watched and listened to the exchanges of the infidel knights? He would attend to Guy later, when he could be assured of no witnesses to the outcome.

Two

He'd noticed the boy some days before, primarily because of his size, and the fact that he wore garb marking him as Guy's property. Since the confrontation in the market place, Miles was plagued with notions of outsmarting his enemy. Now, when he looked at the boy, a plan of sorts formed loosely in his head. An undernourished child, the boy was pathetically paraded in oversized livery that flapped around his skinny frame and restricted his movement. Cast-offs from a previous wretched post-holder perhaps, Miles doubted whether this boy would live long enough to grow into them. Marchant was a man who treated his servants as slaves to be bullied and abused at will. Miles scowled, was there no end to Guy's cruelty? This boy looked barely old enough for the job. Not long from his mother's lap, his pale skin burnished painfully by the intense heat, he had the look of a scared rabbit. Miles watched his faltering progress through the assembled knights. Collecting the occasional backhander from those who wore Guy's colours, the child kept his head down, chin tucked in against his chest as he studiously avoided the malevolent gaze of those who sought out young boys for their own pleasure. Miles feared the child would not last the campaign without someone's intervention.

Ordinarily, a child wouldn't have roused Miles' interest. There were many about, pages and squires who bore beatings and rough handling and contented themselves with dreams of future glory as a knight. As a youngster still tormented by the murder of his own mother, Miles had shared those dreams, had thought of nothing else but acquiring the skills to avenge his mother and vanquish her killer, the Northumbrian baron Gerard-de-Frouville. Many years had passed since he'd landed in Normandy, a gangly youth, with naught but a home-bred horse and a hand-down sword. Now his hands were stained with the blood of others, his skills honed to perfection, and soon he would be in a position to right those wrongs.

First though, there was the small matter of the boy and the more he considered him, the more determined Miles became. Far too many innocents had been lost at the hands of Guy-de-Marchant. It was time to put an end to it, and to him, once and for all. Regardless of what Hugh or Thomas might caution, Miles decided that this boy would not perish at Guy's will.

He raised himself up from the campfire and brushed the sand from his clothes. He was weary, both in body and mind. Injured in the failed attack on Qaqun the previous winter, the endless raids and skirmishes were beginning to take their toll. He marvelled at Hugh's seemingly insatiable energy for the politics of the campaign, while he himself privately longed to return to English shores. He was duty bound to Hugh, but as each new trading vessel moored in the port, his impatience to be away increased. He had much to do and was plagued by the unsettling feeling that time was running out.

"Boy," he called "Spare some water for a battered knight and there'll be a coin in it for you."

The boy stumbled beneath the weight of a large pitcher. Much of the contents had already been lost on the journey from the well and his badly-fitting clothes were soaked. He faltered, casting a furtive eye over his shoulder, no doubt expecting his master or one of his acolytes to leap out and remind him of his duties with a flogging. Men and horses jostled for space, trampling the unwary underfoot.

Miles reached out and yanked the boy from the path of a destrier. The rider's attention was solely on the battle to come rather than Acre's beleaguered inhabitants.

A truce may well have been agreed, but hostilities continued, fuelled in part by mercenaries whose coffers were not yet full. A skirmish outside the city walls had led to a larger conflict and Miles and his men would soon rejoin the fray. Prince Edward's dissatisfaction with the agreement was widely known and he required a swift victory to appease his mood. On this occasion Miles was happy to oblige, he too had need of funds. For now though they took their rest while they awaited Hugh's return.

Hugh-de-Reynard's reputation as a master tactician allowed him entry to the prince's inner circle. Miles knew the tactical meetings could be lengthy affairs as each participant sought to strengthen their position in the future king's eyes by forcing the merit of their particular plan. Hugh had untold patience. He would wait them out and deliver his suggestions when Edward was weary of his minions and ripe for innovation rather than the same old tried and tested politic. Miles had time enough to attend to the matter of the child before Hugh returned to cast doubt on his endeavour.

"I..," the boy shrunk away from Miles' grip. Twisting awkwardly he tried for escape. Fear of another beating quite obvious as he shot a desperate glance around. When it became clear that he could not wriggle free, he gulped a desperate breath and continued. "Please, sir. I...I fetch water for Sir Guy. He is ... impatient."

Thomas, resting by the fire, opened one eye at the mention of Guy's name and gave the boy a cursory inspection. He directed a cautionary shake of the head at Miles as he pulled himself to his feet.

Miles shrugged and reached out for the pitcher. He did not need Thomas overseeing his every move. "Give me the water, and you may seek a second filling for your master. He will wait...or he will answer to me." A smile creased the corners of his mouth as he imagined Guy's reaction to being kept waiting. Guy was a man used to getting his own way, always. It was time he learned the benefits of patience.

The boy however was not smiling. His lower lip trembled. His eyes brimmed wide and wet with tears, but he stood his ground and held fast to the pitcher as if his life depended on it.

Miles admired his courage, even if fear of Guy was at the root of it. "Do not be fearful, child. No one here will harm you." He spread an arm to encompass his small band of cohorts. Thomas obliged with a tight smile, no doubt unwilling to assist Miles in whatever ill-advised plan he was considering, but equally disinclined take out his concerns on a child. "I only seek to slake my thirst and wash the dust from my face," continued Miles pleasantly. "A small service from such a small boy but of great value to me, I can assure you. I shall be in your debt and wouldn't that be a fine thing for you to hold? The favour of a fearless knight, a knight who would be honour bound to come to your aid should you require it."

"Fearless...? Witless more like." Thomas choked back his laughter.

Miles waited, utilising the patience that his enemy sorely lacked, as the boy processed his words, disbelief adding an extra layer of colour to his sun reddened cheeks. The child had no reason to believe him any different to the majority of hardened soldiers who gathered in Acre, Miles knew that, and recognised his uncertainty as he furtively scanned the small company of knights gathered around the fire. The men, in turn, observed their discourse with curiosity, taking their lead from Thomas. Their interest however was short-lived, as they grabbed what succour they could before they were once again thrust into battle. The child avoided eye contact. His narrow features were marred with bruising, some fresh, some yellowed with age. Perhaps sensing Miles' continued scrutiny he scrubbed his sleeve across face, before bowing to the inevitable and offering the pitcher, reluctantly, both the weight and his own hesitancy a barrier to complete compliance.

"Do you have a name?" asked Miles as he reached out further and relieved the boy of his load. "If I am to repay your good deed then I must at the very least, know who I am to serve."

The boy coloured even more. "Some call me Rat or...or... Pig-boy..." Miles nodded. The boy did have a rare stench about him.

"And what does your mother call you?"

"My mother..." The boy's eyes clouded wistfully. "I don't rightly remember... Edmund I suppose."

His voice had the soft burr common to the flat lands of Lincolnshire. Miles wondered at the connection. Coincidence, when it occurred, rarely brought glad tidings. He peered more closely at the child and then, on seeing nothing more than a half starved runt in grubby oversized clothes, he discounted his paranoia. Guy was heir to half of Lincolnshire, his father's fortune made from the ruination of others at the behest of Jewish money lenders. It made sense that he would recruit his household from his own domain.

He quenched his thirst, handed the half empty pitcher back and cupped his hands for the boy to fill them. It was a welcome relief to be rid of desert filth and even the boy seemed more at ease when his face could be clearly seen.

Miles was no devil, but he was in the mood for the devil's work, particularly if it inconvenienced Guy. He smiled at the boy, recalling his own childhood. He too had been a bullied child, belittled and abused at the hands of a rich man's son, but he'd had the wit to engage in verbal defence. This little rat-boy did not.

"Edmund. A fine name. A royal name. Named for Prince Edward's brother are you?" The boy shrugged and Miles doubted he had much knowledge of the royal court beyond King Henry, and his heir. "So, Edmund, what brings you so far from home? I wager Lincoln is more familiar to you than the port of Acre."

In place of an answer the child dropped his chin to his chest and studied his feet.

"Do you miss your home, Edmund? Your family?" The boy merely scuffed at the sand. Miles remembered well enough the bitterness when he'd left the security of his Northumberland home. The circumstances were very different and he'd been almost twice the age of the child before him, but the memory was still fresh – and painful.

"What do you make of life on Crusade? Do you crave to wear the chain and armour and wield a mighty sword? Which shall you be? An honourable Templar or a *despicable* Hospitaller?" He drew a finger across his own throat dramatically and laughed. The boy settled the water jug carefully between his feet and looked up. The smallest of smiles creased his pinched cheeks, in his eyes, a glint of boyish mischief.

"I have skill with the bow," he proudly announced, aping the drawing of a tight string and releasing his imaginary arrow.

Miles grinned back at him. "You must show me with the real thing, Edmund. I have need of a skilled archer."

The bedraggled boy, who barely reached his elbow, now stood proudly, skinny chest puffed out, chin held high and Miles considered his plight afresh. What had begun merely as a way to irritate his rival, had taken a far more sombre tone. The lad was no different to any of the men who wore the white tabard adorned with a red cross. He had dreams. Aspirations which would likely never come to fruition, but would certainly shrivel and die while he remained in Marchant's clutches. Miles sobered immediately and a familiar churning began in his gut. "Does your master treat you well?" he asked.

Behind, Thomas took a step closer as the boy shrugged his thin shoulders. "Miles..."

17

Waving Thomas away Miles continued. "Have you eaten? Duty dictates that I must feed anyone to whom I owe a favour," he smiled, "It is the law, Edmund, I can assure you."

The boy sniffed loudly. His sleeve quickly mopped his nose as he stepped away, but his eyes betrayed him when they strayed to the food enjoyed by the knights.

"I beg yer pardon, sir," he stammered. "The water....Sir Guy... I...must be makin' haste. I'll be headin' for a skelpin' if I drags me feet."

Miles took back the pitcher and with a hand on the boy's shoulder he nudged him in the direction of the well. "Come, little archer, we shall walk together and after the jug is refilled to your master's satisfaction. You may take your fill of our rations." He smiled encouragingly. "I'll not see a future knight or archer starve."

Edmund glanced longingly at the roasted fowl but shook his head. "Nay, m'lord. I must take yer leave. Sir Guy does not wait happily. *There and straight back* - them's me orders. I dare not keep him waitin'."

"It will do him no harm to wait..."

"Miles." Thomas' disapproving tone was more urgent now and as he drew closer the boy's gaze once again slid to his feet. "Do not use the boy for your own ends."

"I do nothing of the sort. You should know me better, Thomas." Miles stooped to the boy, and taking his chin between finger and thumb he encouraged his attention. "If you continue to look at the ground, Edmund, all you will see is dirt. Let me assure you there is more to the world than that. Don't concern yourself with Sir Guy. As I explained, he must deal with me if he has an issue with your punctuality. If he scolds you, tell him you have a protector. Tell him Miles of Wildewood watches over you now."

The boy's eyes grew wide, hopeful and also disbelieving, but before Miles could reassure the lad he was forced to take a hurried step back. A familiar grey destrier forced its way through the crowded courtyard and nudged its way between him and the boy. Hugh-de-Reynard looked down from the saddle. Disapproval creased the older man's face. Even the child shied away and Miles reached out and restrained him with a firm hand at the scruff of his neck.

"Do you consider it wise to taunt your rival?" Hugh asked, his voice low, the question quite rhetorical. Miles knew that he played with fire but all the same he felt the need to defend his actions to his benefactor.

"Do you not see the evidence before you? The boy is hungry. His master does not think to feed him. What would you have me do, allow him to starve? I am simply being charitable. Is that not what you train your knights to be, honourable, charitable?"

Hugh sighed. "There are many boys who grow hungry during this campaign, on both sides of the conflict, yet I do not see you rush to gather them up and provide them with succour. Why is that, Miles? What is so different about this child, I wonder?"

The great horse skittered sideways as a troop of ten or more forced their way past and Hugh maintained control with a muttered word of reassurance to his mount and a curse at the knights who rode their beasts far too recklessly for the densely populated thoroughfares. The boy cowered against Miles leg and he held him there protectively. Many an adult had perished beneath the hooves of the massive beasts; a child would be crushed in an instant.

"There is no difference other than the fact that he is here under my nose," countered Miles as he shouldered Hugh's mount aside, "Still living for now– but for how much longer? I cannot ignore his plight."

"And the fact that he serves Guy-de-Marchant has no bearing on your altruism?"

Miles smiled slyly. "Not at all, though by the sound of him he hails from Lincoln. You remember Lincoln,

Hugh?" The barb was well aimed if a trifle, ill-timed. Hugh scowled his response, but his reply was measured.

"I have nothing but fond memories of Temple Bruer, and so do you, I wager. That is where you made acquaintance with your good friend Thomas, is it not?" Thomas stepped close again, his gaze flicking anxiously between the two men. He placed one hand on the horse's bridle and the other on Miles' arm as if he wished them apart.

"I do not speak of our time at Temple Bruer, I speak of Lincoln," continued Miles. "...as I'm sure you're well aware. The great cathedral, the winding streets, the money lenders..."

Hugh reined the horse closer, leaned down from the saddle and lowered his voice. "You do well to step away now, Miles, lest I remind you of your place. It does not bode well to bring up the past every time you feel the need to vent your spleen. Nor is it wise to rattle the cage of a man such as Guy-de-Marchant. He is well connected as you know, and you do not need me to remind you of his capabilities. Let the child be, and walk away. Your issue with Guy will keep, believe me, you will get your chance. Now is neither the time nor the place."

"Miles, listen well. Hugh speaks with great wisdom." Thomas' voice of reason cut through the tense moment. "Here..." he beckoned to the boy, "There is food aplenty here by the fire. Take your fill and then go. Your master awaits." The boy's dark eyes flicked to the fowl roasting over the fire and the basket of bread and fruit alongside the makeshift hearth. "See, Miles, the boy will be fed, we shall not see him starve, but let him be about his business before he earns a beating for his tardiness. You wish to protect him, a noble act, yet you place him at greater harm by inflaming his master."

Miles glowered at Hugh a moment longer, before the sense of Thomas' words penetrated. Finally, he released the boy and watched as he grabbed a small loaf and darted away through the crowds, ducking under horse's bellies, missing their iron shod hooves by a whisker. In his haste to leave he had taken the food and left the pitcher. Miles weighed the vessel in his hand for a moment. Imagined it bludgeoned against Guy's skull and then shook the image away. He swung his attention back to Hugh. "The boy will not survive without our help, Hugh. You must know that."

"It is a miracle that any of us survive in this land, Miles. I admire your intent, but he is not your concern. You risk far more by engaging Guy in further conflict."

Miles snorted, "I risk nothing. It is you who risk all by consorting with the enemy."

Behind him, Thomas shook his head in disbelief. "Miles, guard your tongue, for pity's sake."

Hugh dismounted and passed the reins to Thomas. "Our young knight does not know the meaning of discretion. I see another lesson looming." He shrugged his frustration. "Take my horse, Thomas, if you please. Prepare the men. We ride out before the sun makes acquaintance with the horizon." He turned to Miles and sighed. "Walk with me, Miles, and perhaps you can explain why you ignore my counsel and insist on goading the man who has the ear of the monarch and the lives of us all in his hands."

Three

From a high spot atop the prince's newly constructed tower, they gazed out above the rooftops and teeming chaos of Acre to the glistening waters of the Mediterranean. Hours before, inland, the horizon had been filled with dust clouds from yet another breach in the truce, a battle that had seen many losses on both sides. Now with the sun at its highest, the extreme temperature had brought with it a languid period of calm. It would not last.

"Miles, I understand your revulsion of Marchant," said Hugh. "Believe me when I say I share it most heartily, but are you willing to risk everything we are sworn to protect, simply to settle a score?"

Miles shrugged belligerently. He admired Hugh and accepted that in most matters his counsel was sound and indeed sought after. But he couldn't shake the feeling that on this occasion, he was being carefully manipulated and manoeuvred out of the way for some greater purpose that he was not yet privy to.

"I see no risk. Guy remains unaware of our role."

"Guy suspects and that is enough to make him dangerous. He has the ear of those who quite naturally favour barons above bastards and has the sense to use what little he does know to influence the court against us."

"You're mistaken, Hugh. This is personal. It is less about what we did or didn't do at Edward's behest and more about who we are - who I am. Whether it ends here and now, or out there on some Godforsaken battlefield it will not abate until either he or I are beaten."

"And the boy?"

"What about the boy?"

"Do you simply use him to goad your rival, to encourage a reaction, or is there more to this?"

"You know there's more."

"Is that not personal also? I am not blind. I see what you see, Miles. When I look at that child I too am reminded of another young boy. It is not so long ago since you came to me in need of protection. I understand your affinity with this child, Guy is a cruel master, the child is vulnerable, but I wonder whether your own need for revenge against the Frouvilles, is colouring your decision-making in this instance."

Miles scuffed the toe of his boot at the sand, just as Edmund had done earlier. The irony was not lost on him. As always Hugh's astuteness was unquestionable. Despite Miles' hatred of Guy and everything he stood for, he was nevertheless, simply target practice, a means to an end, an additional opportunity to hone his skills in preparation for the day when he finally came face to face with Gerard-de-Frouville, his mother's killer. If he were honest, he would admit that every man he had killed in battle thus far had been training for the day when he would put a sword through Frouville's heart.

He raised his head and studied the man before him. "Perhaps," he admitted, "but the motive for my intervention is not the issue here. The child will never grow to be a man without a protector, just as I would have perished were it not for you. I repay your kindness by protecting the boy, do you not see that?"

Hugh frowned. "And what of Guy? How do you expect to rectify this matter? The boy belongs to him, whether it suits you or not. What do you intend, a knife between his ribs in the dead of night?"

Miles gave a dismissive shrug. "If that's what it takes. Guy is no stranger to the blade. It's the least he deserves."

"Maybe, but murder the son of a wealthy baron and you will pay with your life. He is protected by law - the king's law. You are sworn to uphold that law."

"I also fight for a Christian God, but I see no sign of his benevolence in this place."

"Miles," hissed Hugh. "Consider your words before they fall into the wrong ears. I cannot protect you when you are hell bent on blasphemy and self-destruction."

"What then do you suggest?" muttered Miles. "I am thwarted at every turn. I seek only to protect an innocent, yet the one who should be punished is protected instead."

"Negotiation is a far more powerful weapon than you allow, Miles. How do you imagine great wars are won and treaties made? The greater strength of force may win the battle, but lasting peace is created through negotiation."

"I do not seek lasting peace with Guy."

"Guy's family have great sway with Edward. Edward will soon be king. We must think to the future – always."

Miles snorted his frustration. Of course Hugh made sense, but that did not negate his desire to be rid of the man whose predilection for dark deeds was growing unchecked. "Guy will not negotiate. He is an indulged brat grown to dangerous man."

"If he suspects your interest, he will capitalise on that and the boy will suffer further."

"Then I have no option but to take the boy, Guy will demand his return and this will be settled one way or another."

"I did not save you from a Frouville sword only to lose you to Marchant's. You are too impulsive, Miles. I too would wish to vanquish all those who have erred against me? And let me tell you there are many. But I do not choose to openly display my ire, for to do so is to weaken my position. Hold fast, Miles. Evil and dark deeds abound. Within this very stronghold there are those who would work against our cause, against the monarch. If we are wise we might yet use their evil against them."

Miles nodded slowly. He too had been aware of a subtle shift in allegiances, the balance of power tipping ever so slightly, defeats where victories had been guaranteed. Edward's reluctance to sign Baybars' truce had left his position in Acre unstable and the prince was rightly concerned, hence the hurried meetings and his increased reliance on Hugh. Perhaps there was another, less confrontational way to trap Guy and although a confrontation appealed to his current mood, he accepted that might not be beneficial to the child. "What do you know of dark deeds?" he eventually asked.

"Enough. I have my sources."

"Is that why you visit Baybars' harem in the dead of night and risk a traitor's death?"

Hugh's laughter rumbled from deep within. "Harem? Miles, abstinence, or I suspect in your case the lack of it, has gone to your head. I think you mistake me for Thomas. Is he not the ladies' man among us? If you must blacken my name then for pity's sake, make it believable. At the risk of disappointing all the hot-blooded young men in Acre, I can assure you there is no nest of wanton wenches out there in the desert, and there's not a man here, including my enemies, who would accept that I stand at Baybars' right hand, either for want of a woman or for political discourse."

Of course Hugh was right, Miles knew that with a certainty borne of long acquaintance, nevertheless, the man frequently left the safety of Acre and journeyed into the desert. Miles had observed his departure on more nights than he cared to recall and despite Hugh's declaration, there *was* talk that could not be denied. Perhaps those who stood by Hugh's side, when in Edward's company, would not speak aloud of their suspicions, but privately they wondered about this educated, worldly man, a man with dubious provenance, and more importantly, the ear of the future king. There were many who were concerned at Hugh's uncanny ability to influence.

"Why then do you cross enemy lines, if not to court the Sultan or seek comfort with a maiden?"

Hugh shook his head. "I do not further my cause by explaining my every action to a man who has not yet learned his place. Trust me, Miles. I work for England and the king."

"And Guy?"

"Guy works for no man but himself. He is a flea on the back of England's lion, and he must be treated with care. Scratch him not, for you may simply spread his pox." Hugh glanced around and when confident they were alone he lowered his voice. "Edward's refusal to sign the treaty has angered Sultan Baybars. He grows weary with our English prince. I fear retaliation."

"Retaliation? In what way? He will break his own truce if he attacks Acre."

"There are more subtle methods to rid oneself of an irritation."

Miles sobered. It seemed more was at stake than his feud with Guy, and like Hugh and all those who rode with him, Miles' allegiance was to the future king. It seemed that the boy's plight must by necessity, wait another day. "How can I assist?" he asked.

"Can you be trusted to keep your head and hold your tongue?"

"Of course. Do I give you cause to doubt that?"

"Constantly, Miles," sighed Hugh, "but I value your loyalty above all others." He reached out, cuffing Miles roughly about the head. "We ride out soon, a sortie to replenish the cattle taken from us, a further opportunity to remind the sultan that we remain, when he would have us gone. Thomas will take my place and lead the men. We must pay a visit elsewhere. We shall be back by nightfall, time enough to attend to the matter of the child."

"You agree, then – about the boy?"

"I did not disagree, Miles. I merely take issue with your methods. No matter, first we will attend to more pressing affairs and then we shall endeavour to negotiate a favourable outcome for the lad."

"Whom do you seek?" asked Miles as he and Hugh skirted the main body of men and headed west into the desert.

"A man who has news of St George-de-Lebeyre."

Miles frowned. "The raid is long since past. Why do you dwell on old news?"

"Because all is not as it seems. Edward's plot was hexed by another. I cannot accept that an entire raiding party were felled by the heat and rancid vittals."

Miles pulled his horse closer, intrigued by the notion that the audacious raid, a mere twelve miles from Acre, had been thwarted by a more devious hand. He knew that Hugh had provided the intelligence behind the raid and although successful in terms of results, the severe debilitation of the men had increased underlying suspicion of Hugh's strategy. It made sense then that Hugh would seek to exonerate himself and uncover the true culprit, if such a person truly existed.

"It was uncommonly hot," countered Miles, "and the men were newly arrived and unused to the cuisine. It's possible that bad luck, rather than sabotage was the mistress responsible."

"Luck is a fickle bedfellow, that is certainly true, but in this case I'm convinced the answer lies elsewhere."

Hugh pushed his horse on, leaving Miles to follow and as they continued in silence Miles wondered about the integrity of the man they were to meet, a person who'd held information vital to the campaign for almost a year, and was only now persuaded to part with it. He couldn't believe that Hugh was foolish enough to walk blindly into

27

a trap, but all the same he maintained a high level of caution.

When, on arrival, they were greeted not by a furtive seller of secrets from Baybars' camp, but by a dusky beauty who flashed her lashes and a coy smile, Miles shot a knowing look at Hugh. Harem or not, this was certainly a wanton wench. Thomas would be mightily aggrieved that he had missed the opportunity to join them.

He studied the woman discreetly through half closed lashes, as he attempted to filter out the cloying incense, and while she set about providing refreshments. She was indeed a beauty, and despite Hugh's protestation to the contrary, it appeared she had more than secrets on her mind. Her eyes darted back and forth between the task at hand and the older knight. When Miles caught her attention, her full lips twitched into an instant smile and her eyes lit with mischief. Hugh cleared his throat impatiently.

"Jesmina, please allow me to introduce my companion, Miles of Wildewood, a good and trusted man. You may speak openly before him and in my stead you may deal directly with him."

Jesmina tipped her head in acknowledgement.

"Miles, may I present Jesmina. Her father, Saladin, has information of great importance, and has agreed at some considerable risk to himself and his family, to share that information with us."

Miles smiled. Now he wasn't sure. Was it the woman or the information that Hugh sought?" He flicked his gaze between the two, but could not decide who played the cleverer game. Jesmina fluttered her lashes at him, as if she read his thoughts.

"My father is delayed," she murmured, as she returned her attention to Hugh. "His services are required elsewhere this evening."

"Elsewhere?" Hugh grunted his annoyance while Jesmina merely smiled indulgently, reaching out to pat his shoulder in a familiar and consolatory way. Miles watched with some amusement as Hugh's attention lingered for a moment on her hand. He wondered once more at their relationship and the number of times Hugh had made this journey.

"The Sultan holds counsel. Father was unable to decline attendance."

"Did he leave a message perhaps? We have come at great risk – not only to ourselves." The underlying threat, beneath Hugh's measured words was obvious to Miles and it immediately banished any frivolous thoughts he may have entertained about Hugh and the seductress. Hugh may well be tempted by the woman but he was not beguiled. He had business to attend to and as Miles knew all too well he would not be diverted by anything, no matter how tempting.

Jesmina narrowed her eyes at Hugh's tone. "I have what *the Fox* seeks," she lingered over his soubriquet in a way that suggested to Miles that Hugh might well have enjoyed her on previous occasions, but tonight she was patently wasting her time."

"Then, madam, I shall relieve you of that onerous burden and leave you in peace." Hugh cast an eye to the tent flap, and considered for a moment, as if concerned at the turn of events and anxious to be away. Perhaps the absence of Saladin and mention of Baybars' war counsel gave him cause for suspicion, but Miles could see no imminent threat, other than to Hugh's debateable vow of celibacy and he raised a questioning brow at his offhand manner. Surely Hugh would have more success if he were to charm the lady. He was certainly capable. It was to Thomas' continuing dismay that the older knight seemed to carry more allure for the ladies of Acre than he did himself. Miles found the whole issue entertaining and as it provided yet another incident with which to taunt his good friend, he settled back to see how Hugh planned to extricate himself. As if attuned to Miles' thoughts, Hugh returned his attention to the young woman and smiled.

"We cannot dally this evening, Jesmina...more's the pity. If I were alone, it would be a different matter." He shot Miles a conspiratorial look. "We are on a mission of great urgency and need the item promised by your father without further delay."

Jesmina, apparently appeased by Hugh's contriteness, reached into her ample cleavage and fished around for, what seemed to Miles, a considerable time. Either she had many items concealed about her person or was in need of help to retrieve them. Miles could think of worse ways to spend an evening and would have happily obliged with assistance, though he suspected Hugh may have taken umbrage at that.

"Is that it?" asked Miles as they made their way back to Acre under cover of darkness. "A single glass vial? How does that solve the riddle of St George-de-Lebeyre?"

Hugh patted the precious cargo, now nestled at his own breast. "If you wished to thwart a raiding party and defeat a group of experienced soldiers, how would you go about it, Miles?"

"I would engage them in battle."

"And if you did not wish your colours to be known?"

Miles shrugged. "I would take the colours of my enemy."

"Ah, yes. I forget, you are quite the spy, are you not, Miles."

"Sometimes it is prudent to create an illusion to protect the primary aim." Miles narrowed his eyes. "I learn from a master."

"Exactly. The men at St George-de-Lebeyre, are a prime example of a most effective illusion. They did not fall prey to the effects of heat or rancid food, although it must be said, both were reasonable conclusions given the time of year and the appalling table manners of the raiding party."

"*You* planned the raid."

Hugh shrugged. "True."

"And Edward led it."

Hugh grinned, "And *his* table manners are of course exemplary"

"So, if not a result of bad planning ...what?"

"Our men were poisoned."

"Poisoned? Why?"

"Perhaps the aim was to kill and the assailants misjudged the dose, or perhaps the intention was merely to throw doubt on my abilities as a tactician. Edward suffered an embarrassment. If it were not for past success I may well have been ousted. Indeed I might yet be – removed."

"But poison? How do you know this?"

Hugh grimaced. "I have some expertise in this matter and now, courtesy of Saladin, I have a sample of the poison used. Someone else in Edward's company has a similar knowledge. He seeks to eradicate the future king – or the future king's advisor. Either way we must seek him out to get to the truth."

"Saladin was unable to provide a name along with his poison?"

"I had hoped that he might be persuaded but I fear Saladin's absence from our rendezvous suggests a greater power has influence over him."

"Baybars?"

"Perhaps."

"But you suspect Guy?"

Hugh turned in the saddle and frowned. "Miles your obsession with Guy is clouding your vision. He is not the only suspect."

"Yet you include him in your suspicion?"

"Not directly, he has too much to lose. His family are linked to the king in ways which are beyond our current understanding. He would not risk his father's wrath by jeopardising that relationship. I believe he may have knowledge of the incident, simply because he associates with men of dubious morals, but I need proof and I need you to hold your tongue and curtail your animosity for the man until my investigation is complete. Whoever did this threatens England and the Crown."

Four

Thomas awaited Miles on his return. His grave expression had naught to do with the recent raid. The aroma of roasted meat was proof enough that the raid had been successful. Yet the tense atmosphere around the camp was enough to alert Miles that all was not well.

"Miles, I have ill news." Thomas held up a placatory hand as Miles reined in his horse. "The boy has not been seen. I fear Guy may have learned of your interest and disposed of the lad."

"What!" Miles slid from his horse, anger and fear warring inside. He shot a furious glance at Hugh's retreating back. He should have tended to the matter before his jaunt to visit the buxom Jesmina. He should not have been persuaded to delay. After all, his attendance had not been necessary, merely a ploy by Hugh to distract him from his feud with Guy. If the lad had perished as a result, then Guy would not suffer alone.

"How do you know?" He reached out, clutched tightly to Thomas' jerkin and pulled him closer. Thomas reacted swiftly, gripping Miles' fist and squeezing it firmly, his irritation at Miles aggression betrayed by the slight tick at the corner of his eye. He was bigger, older and a far more experienced soldier than Miles and despite his usual amiable demeanour was not about to allow Miles' undisciplined behaviour.

"Be careful your temper does not herald your own downfall, Miles. Do not strike the hand that feeds you or the sword that watches your back. Be still for pity's sake, *we* are not your enemies."

Miles dropped his hand and dragged in a lungful of Acre's night air. "Just tell me what happened."

"He was here, earlier, looking for you..."

"Edmund?"

"No, Guy. He left you this." Thomas held out a small grubby cap, of the type the lad had worn earlier in the day. There was no knowing if it was Edmund's or whether it belonged to one of the older boys in Guy's service. The implication, however, was obvious. "He laughed. You know how he is. He's goading you, Miles, as we knew he would. You should have left the child alone. He is in more danger now than ever before."

Miles did not need the reminder of his folly. His gut twisted because of it. "Has anyone seen the boy, since he brought the water?" Miles directed his question beyond Thomas to the men behind him, all wary now as they realised that the plight of the young boy might well be the catalyst that finally threw them all into bloody dispute with a man they all despised. They answered in the negative. No one had seen the child. One by one they gathered their weapons and stood ready.

"Then perhaps Guy can enlighten me." Miles snatched up the water jug left behind by Edmund and pushed his way past Thomas.

"Miles, wait. Wait for Hugh." Thomas followed, his attempts to restrain Miles cast roughly aside.

"Hugh meets with Edward. He has matters of state to discuss. I can deal with Guy." He turned abruptly and noticed for the first time, the concern of the men who awaited his orders, who were ready to support him in whatever madness he planned. He sobered instantly. He could not drag them with him into certain conflict. He owed them more than that. They, along with Thomas and Hugh had extricated him from countless messes of his own making and would do so again in an instant, but this was

34

personal. It went beyond the boy, Edmund, back to Lincoln and a dark deed not yet atoned for. At some stage they would all pay, but not today.

He shot an apologetic glance at his good friend. "Thomas, worry not, all will be well. I will not jeopardise what we hold dear. I simply seek the child."

"Guy expects you to react just as you have done, with recklessness. Do not make yourself an easy target, you must temper your impulsiveness and outwit him instead."

Miles nodded. He'd spent his youth outwitting his nemesis Gerard-de-Frouville. But could he do it again with Guy?

The water vessel hung from his hand and he swung it back and forth, testing its weight and judging the damage it would cause if it were by chance to be dashed against the skull of his enemy. The thought occupied him as he made his way through the murk of night-time Acre towards Guy's enclave. Despite the hour Guy was waiting, though his appearance suggested that he was not long from his bed or his latest woman. A man who ordinarily cared a great deal about his own facade, he was not usually seen in such disarray. Miles took some pleasure from the knowledge that perhaps it was his own arrival that scuffed his enemy's veneer.

"Yours I believe." He swung the jug, and Guy, caught unawares, fumbled the catch and the vessel smashed at his feet. The remains of the water soaked his hastily donned garments. He attempted to cover his obvious annoyance with a smug smile, but his tightly clenched fists, hinted at his true demeanour. Miles smiled. The first blood in this battle was definitely his.

"It seems you covet more than a pitcher, Miles." Guy kicked the shattered jug aside. "Always you yearn for things that do not belong to you, an unfortunate trait which will no doubt have equally unfortunate consequences."

Miles had no patience for Guy's verbal games. He narrowed his eyes and assessed his rival.

"You talk in riddles, Guy. Explain yourself."

"The rat-boy. The runt who stinks of horse piss and camel dung, he tells me a fine knight seeks to take him away. I ask 'which knight?', for there are no *fine* knights left in Acre, simply armoured demons corrupted by war and greed."

"Speak for yourself, Guy. Beyond your own cesspit of an enclave there are many who hold chivalry and honour above personal gain."

Guy's face twisted into an ugly frown. "But not you, Miles. Not you. We both know that is far from the truth in your case – don't we?"

"Where is the boy?"

"*My* boy. *My* property."

Miles recalled Hugh's words and Thomas' caution and chose his words with care. "I am here to negotiate a price for him."

"Negotiate? Guy sniggered. You have spent too long in *The Fox's* company methinks. I wager negotiation is the last thing you wish for. Tell me, Miles, what do you have to trade for the lad? What do you have that I could possibly want?" He cocked his head, goading Miles further."

Miles gritted his teeth and wished for Hugh's patience. He had many things to trade – a sharp blade, a well aimed arrow, but Guy would want neither of those. "Name your price."

"You have funds?" Guy's disbelief in Miles solvency was clear.

"More than you think." Miles lips twitched briefly as he thought of the treasures he had accumulated during his twelve months on Crusade. The spoils of war, funds needed for his return to England. He had no intention of trading them.

"You surprise me, Miles, but alas all the treasure in the world will not save the lad. You are too late. The boy is gone."

"Gone?" Miles straightened, his hand strayed to the dagger at his belt and, behind Guy, men appeared from the shadows. Men still stained from battle, and blurred with drink, harbingers who reeked of death. They watched him with an unhealthy anticipation, like feral dogs come upon a lamb, but Miles was not about to be slaughtered.

Guy shrugged dismissively. "I have no use for a child who cannot learn. A weakling who struggles with the simplest of tasks. A boy who is disloyal to his master."

One step forward brought Miles within striking distance, but it was matched by the dark guards who stood to attention. A glint of metal in firelight was a subtle warning to tread carefully. Miles had no illusions; they would cut him down without a care and go about their business while his body rotted underfoot. These black-hearted mercenaries claimed to be fighting for Christianity, in truth they were the devil incarnate.

"What have you done with the boy?" he demanded.

Guy's lips twitched into a sly smile. "Me? Why nothing - yet. The boy has run off, slipped his tether and disappeared. I hold you responsible, *fine knight*, and when I catch him and hang him, as I most surely will, you may watch. In fact, I insist that you do. Perhaps that will teach you the perils of interfering in my affairs..." He left the last words hanging, a subtle threat, but Miles was beyond subtlety and snarled his response.

"If you have harmed him in any way - I will..."

"You will what? Do you forget who I am? What I represent? The power I hold? You cannot touch me, Miles, and although it may pain you greatly - you know this to be true."

"I want the boy, Guy."

"You want many things, Miles. None of which are within your reach. No title, no land, no credibility. You are a bastard upstart and the sooner you realise your position in life and take up your pitchfork or plough, the better for all."

"I want the boy," repeated Miles. His words steady, his state of mind less so, his body wound so tight, he found it difficult to recall Thomas' words of caution let alone act upon them. He squeezed the hilt of his dagger to alleviate his desire to plunge the weapon into Guy's self-righteous, smirking face.

"Then seek him in the dark streets where the flesh traders lurk," hissed Guy, "or out there in the desert among the hot sands and rotting bodies. Or...perhaps I jest and he is not lost at all but merely hidden from view."

Miles sprang forward; caution thrust aside, negotiation now merely a word to choke upon. There was only one way to deal with a man like Guy-de-Marchant. He drew the dagger, the tip almost at his rival's throat, the reward of blood a mere hairs breadth away, but the prize was snatched from him when he was pummelled sideways by one of the henchmen.

He hit the ground with the full weight of his armoured assailant on his chest, his arm yanked sideways and held immobile as his wrist was stamped upon by another, the dagger skittering out of reach.

Guy stepped closer, swagger and bravado transforming him instantly into a puff-chested caricature. "I could just kill you now," he shrilled, his excitement at Miles' restraint and sudden vulnerability colouring his cheeks unpleasantly. "And believe me I would savour the moment and suffer no consequences for my action. You swear allegiance to the wrong side, Miles. Hugh's current position of favour with Edward is short-lived, soon he, and all the *fine knights* who ride with him will be seeking another patron." Guy nodded to the man whose arm threatened Miles' windpipe and the pressure increased significantly. As Miles struggled for breath, Guy raised a hand and beckoned a second man from the shadows. The man dipped his head, listening intently as Guy whispered urgently.

"Consider it done, my lord," the man replied with a sly grin in Miles' direction.

"Release, him." Guy barked the command at those who held Miles captive. As the weight was removed Miles struggled to his feet, frustration fuelling a need to lash out, whatever the consequences. He squared up to the man who had stamped on his wrist, but he was rewarded with no more than a snarl. The dogs would not give him the satisfaction of a fair fight.

Guy circled him as if he were a specimen to be ogled or a slave to be assessed. "Miles, a word of advice, listen well. Forget the boy; he is as good as dead. You and I however have a score to settle and be assured it will be done before I leave this accursed place. Run back to the high and mighty Reynard. Tell him I have not forgotten Lincoln. I will never forget Lincoln and God help me neither will you."

Miles had no intention of relaying Guy's message. He had no wish for Hugh to learn of his ill-advised negotiations and indeed had more pressing matters to attend to. The man who Guy had commanded in hushed tones had mounted his horse and was headed out of camp. One of those who shared a privileged position within Guy's militia, he had already come to Miles' attention. His barbaric behaviour with enemy prisoners had earned him an infamous reputation. Miles shuddered to think that he might have knowledge of the child's disappearance. The hired man's obvious amusement and gratification at the plight of others sealed his fate as far as Miles was concerned. One missing boy may be of no great importance amidst the theatre of war, but Miles wondered at Guy's reaction should his favoured man also disappear.

Common sense dictated that if he were unable to include Hugh in his latest confidence then he should at least seek out Thomas to accompany him. There was great risk involved in heading out alone into Baybars' territory, after dark, particularly in pursuit of one under Guy's command. Thomas was capable, fearless and possessed the self-control which Miles accepted he frequently lacked himself. Thomas should go with him, he knew that, but he had not the time to visit every willing maid in order to locate him. He hesitated only long enough to mount his own horse. He could not delay. The child could well be strapped to the mercenary's saddle, bound and gagged and headed for a sandy grave, or worse, a sale to one of the many tribesmen who bartered for anything and anyone. An innocent child, a virgin girl, a measure of opium, or a team of stinking camels, there was no difference in this land.

He followed with every intention to recover the boy and strip Guy of his henchman by whatever means necessary.

Guy it seemed had other plans.

Less than a mile from Acre's walls, alone and guided merely by star-light, Miles lost sight of his quarry. Half a mile further on, he rediscovered the man, now supported by four of his cohorts. He could not believe his own stupidity. Despite turning his horse and pushing the beast to its limit, he could not outrun them. Hugh's words of caution echoed impotently in his ears. He should have listened. He should have accepted his council. Unfortunately he had not.

Five

It was simply a matter of time. Sooner or later something must yield, the rope suspending him perilously above the snake pit, or his own resolve. Miles was reluctant to wager the outcome as neither provided for a satisfactory outcome. The endless desert night, with its plummeting temperatures, had mocked the earlier burning heat of the day while the unearthly call of creatures lurking in the darkness had tormented him continually. He'd cursed their banshee wails, but accepted that without them he would have succumbed to exhaustion and surely slipped to his death. Now, as slender fingers of daylight taunted through the rock fissures, the snakes beneath his feet became restless. Caressed into wakefulness by the morning sun they uncoiled their bodies and scented the air. Miles had dared not sleep with a noose tight at his neck, and so for him there was no gentle morning-time caress, no languid stretch alongside silken scented skin, merely the harsh reminder that as a new day dawned, his torturers would return.

Guy - Miles vowed there and then that he would see him dead.

It was reckless of course, imagining he could get the better of Guy-de-Marchant without a considered plan and sufficient men to back him up. But where Guy was concerned, common sense had a habit of deserting him. His current predicament was a direct result of his impulsiveness, and the certain knowledge that he was complicit in his own downfall merely added to the grimness of the situation.

Miles teetered precariously on a narrow wooden stake driven into a hole in the floor of the cave. With a circumference barely large enough for one foot he risked disaster, and the bite of the noose, each time he shifted his weight from right foot to left. His muscles ached from maintaining the rigid stance, while behind his back he worked impotently with frozen fingers in an attempt to unravel the knotted twine that bound his wrists.

Miles cursed aloud. Guy - he should have killed him back in Lincoln when he had the chance, and would have if it were not for the counsel of the older and wiser Hugh. There was so much he did not understand about the recent past, the dark deeds and his own part in them, nor did he fully comprehend Hugh's reticence. However he knew with certainty that despite Hugh's caution, Guy would ultimately pay for the evil that consumed the man and threatened them all. Either God or a sharp blade would demand his ultimate penitence. Miles favoured the blade.

The sound of approaching horses dragged Miles from thoughts of Guy's eventual demise, back to what was feasible, given his current situation, and he tensed in readiness for what was to come. He had borne the earlier beating with little option, outnumbered and held fast as he was by Guy's clever ambush. Unwilling to take the life of an English knight in plain sight of witnesses he had merely used Miles' own reckless nature against him. He knew Miles would follow the bait and he had, and landed himself directly into the hands of men for whom torture was an entertainment. Struggling impotently when they'd tightened the rope at his neck, they'd merely laughed, hauling on the rope until he swung, feet from the ground. He'd dangled in mid-air for a moment, kicking desperately until his feet found purchase on the narrow stake. He would not easily forget the panic as the stricture tightened.

Nor would he easily forget his own foolishness in ignoring his own caution and not seeking Thomas' help.

His impulsiveness had merely placed the child in more danger. The boy might well be imprisoned elsewhere or already dead. Miles swallowed the bile that rose in his throat at his own impotency. Despite his courage in battle he felt apprehension curdle inside as he listened to the jingle of harness and approaching footsteps. But it was not Guy's returning henchmen who finally appeared at the cave mouth.

"So this is where you are hiding. Myself, I prefer the company of a warm wench to a pit of writhing serpents..." Thomas' dry tone drew a measure of relief from Miles. Both humour and impatience, borne from long acquaintance, oiled each syllable like the mechanism of some great trebuchet. Miles smiled sourly and prepared for the inevitable verbal assault. It had been folly to assume he could outsmart such a shrewd knight. Just as *he* had followed Guy's bait, Thomas had obviously dogged his footsteps, a little late to prevent his assault but most welcome nonetheless. Another hour and the sun's rays were destined to fill the entire crevice and he would have roasted like a pig on a spit.

Miles inclined his head awkwardly. Many hours strung up like a game-bird, meant movement was restricted and painful. Thomas' laconic smile and raised brow coaxed a frustrated snort in response. The man was obviously set to make the most of Miles' predicament.

"You took your time," Miles croaked. "Your skill with a sharp blade would be most welcome now. And if you possess a skin of water or a plan of escape, you'd best share them also. My throat is as dry as a camel's behind and we have an urgent need to be gone from this place."

Thomas propped himself against the cave mouth and tutted loudly. As the sound ricocheted, the snakes swung their heads in alarm, a hundred or more forked tongues flicking in unison.

"Water I have aplenty. However, a plan? Nay, Miles, after all, y*ou* are the planner, are you not? This...." he gestured vaguely to the rock prison, the snakes, and lastly to Miles' perilous position. "This...is part of *your* plan I assume?"

Above his head, thick knotted rope secured Miles to an ancient timber, crudely wedged against the uneven rock walls. He dare not lift his head to assess its weight bearing potential. Perhaps if Thomas were to climb its length to reach the rope, the timber would fracture and they would both tumble to the snake ridden floor. Not a favourable outcome, but marginally better than his current situation. He swallowed a sharp retort and glowered at Thomas instead.

"Remind me, Miles," continued Thomas, his mirth at Miles' discomfort evident. "Were you not intent on outwitting Guy? From your current predicament I deduce you were not entirely successful."

Miles grunted. He'd had a belly full of Thomas' jibes. The fact that his brother-in-arms was right to question his judgement was neither here nor there. He certainly hadn't intended his foray into Sultan Baybars' territory to end on such a poor note. And he was certainly glad that Thomas' curiosity had ensured his timely arrival. But the man's delight at his misfortune did nothing to lighten his mood. Once he was free he would wipe that infernal grin from Thomas' face once and for all.

"All will be well...you said."

"And so it is...," Miles hissed. He took a breath, and wriggled his frozen fingers until he was able to feel a loosening of the knot. The pressure on his pinioned shoulders was immense. He swayed, balanced precariously with one outstretched leg and finally righted himself.

"Take care, my young hawk. It would be unwise to slip from your perch," cautioned Thomas. Miles glowered back at him, but the man simply leaned in closer and continued. "What brings you out here amid Baybars' horde and against Hugh's direct orders, I wonder?" He smiled knowingly. "Ah but wait, let me guess. All that talk of the sultan's harem has obviously addled your brain. Could that be the answer to this puzzle? Is that why you risk the wrath of your benefactor and the loss of your life...for a wench? "

"Cut me loose."

"All in good time, Miles. Let me savour the moment a little longer. Be glad that it is I come to save your hide and not Hugh, or you would be taking your chances with Baybars."

"Strange as it may seem to you, Hugh does not control my every action," grunted Miles.

"No? Then perhaps he should. Your foolhardiness will be the death of you, Miles. Admit it. One smile and the promise of more and any harlot has the better of you - and if we don't make haste I fear we will both pay the price for your lechery."

"*I fear* you confuse your own low morals with mine – *friend*. Believe what you will, however this has less to do with a woman and more to do with a missing child. You chose to sit around the campfire filling your belly. I chose to act to thwart some dark deed. If that is foolhardy then I bow to your greater wisdom – or at least I will, when you cut the rope and release me."

"Your gratitude is overwhelming Miles. Next time I ponder on whether to save your skin, I shall leave you to the snakes...and Baybars."

"I did not ask for your assistance."

"True, your first mistake. I follow at Hugh's bidding, to keep you from further harm. I see you full of righteous indignation, determined to beat a man who plays games that have no rules, and what am I to think? When you do not return, when you disappear just like the poor child you seek, I have no option but to search every nook and cranny, every cave and Bedouin tent. It seems once again I am burdened with nursemaid duties."

"Pah, nursemaid indeed! You thought you'd follow my lead to Baybars' harem. Your reputation precedes you, Thomas, and although I'll admit it has been some time since we were in the company of *fine* ladies, you do me ill to suggest that my mind is as consumed as yours with thoughts of the opposite sex."

Thomas' guffaw echoed around them. "You're not wrong, Miles. With the exception of the exquisite Eleanor, Edward's attendees leave a lot to be desired, harlots and camp followers who have likely shared their pleasures with both sides of the campaign. However, as I said, I followed to keep you from the perils of your own making. Guy's man was seen leaving Acre shortly after your attempted negotiation with Guy. He returned. You did not. It has taken more than a little persuasion for him to reveal your location."

"He still lives?"

"He shall not ride at Guy's right arm again."

Miles smiled slyly.

"Hold fast, Miles. This is not the time to stir the pot of revenge with Guy. Hugh will no doubt stress the same upon our return. He warned you, Miles. You did not listen."

Miles snorted. "Revenge? I have not yet begun. The child is still in his possession, I'm sure of it. We must locate him."

Thomas raised a brow. "We? Ah so now you seek my help. What of yesterday, when you decided that you could tackle Guy yourself?"

"I was wrong."

"I'm glad you see that, Miles. Let's hope the child is not the victim of your error."

Miles swallowed the guilt that threatened to overwhelm him. Thomas could not berate him any more than he berated himself. "Might I suggest that we continue this discussion later - after you release me?"

"Perhaps I'll leave you here a little longer. Maybe that will teach you to share your plans"

"For pity's sake, Thomas, I had no time. The boy was being taken by Guy's man. If I had stopped to seek your help I could not have followed."

"You saw the boy?"

"No, but the intent was clear."

"What is clear to *me* is that Guy wanted rid of a troublesome knight and his ploy almost worked. The boy is not out here in a shallow grave, nor is he tied to a camel and headed for the flesh markets."

"How can you be sure? He could be anywhere."

Thomas skirted the edge of the cave, avoiding the serpents with care, and with some effort scaled the rough rock wall until he was level with the beam. He withdrew his knife and leaned forward from his perch, teetering for a moment before he was able to grab the rope above Miles head. He placed the tip of the blade, not at the rough twine, but at the stubble beneath Miles' chin. He smiled. "You should have trusted Hugh."

Miles swayed and the rope at his throat tightened alarmingly. He did not share Thomas' amusement.

"Hugh...always Hugh."

"If it were not for Hugh, you'd have met your end in Northumberland at the tip of Frouville's sword. He only means to protect you. Lord knows why, you are more trouble than you are surely worth. What possessed you to chase off alone into enemy territory?"

"I chase no one. I followed a child beater, fell victim to a gang of men who sully England's good name and in the process stumbled upon something that will no doubt go some way to recover my position with Hugh."

"Enlighten me, Miles. Though I fear the knowledge will not please me."

"The rope?" reminded Miles.

"I'm waiting?"

Miles forced a grim smile. "Saladin the Snake Master."

47

Sliding an anxious glance at the slithering mass below them, Thomas leaned closer. "The poison trader?"

"The very one."

What does he have to do with a beaten child?"

"Perhaps nothing, but this is his cave. These are his snakes and Guy has knowledge of both."

"I see," said Thomas, though clearly he did not. "Does this have anything to do with Hugh's current investigation?"

"You know the detail of it?"

"I know, as you do, that he visits Baybars' harem rather more regularly than is wise."

Miles grinned. Thomas was yet another convinced at the harem's existence. He chose not to disappoint him for the moment. "I suspect there may be a more obvious reason for his visit."

"A woman?"

"Indeed, the beauty known as Jesmina. But that aside, darker forces are at work...and still are."

"I see." Thomas mulled the information slowly and Miles dangled while he waited. "You didn't come here to solve a riddle for Hugh though, did you?" muttered Thomas as he sawed through the rope, releasing Miles to plummet to the stone floor.

"Not specifically, no," grunted Miles as he scrambled to his feet, his hands still tied behind his back, his neck raw from the rope. "I came to save a child and I have failed miserably." He swung his gaze back and forth as he debated his next step. The snakes hissed their annoyance at his intrusion and one or two made half-hearted strikes. Fortunately the sun had not yet fuelled them for battle.

Thomas slid from his rocky perch and joined Miles, swinging his sword to ward off the writhing mass. "Perhaps not a total failure."

Miles gestured to the expanse of the empty cave. "I do not see the boy, do you? There is mischief and plotting afoot and no amount of peace-making by Egypt's Sultan or

Jerusalem's King, will negate it. In the midst of it all who is there to care about the fate of a peasant boy who longs to be an archer. He is lost, Thomas, and I blame myself for that."

Thomas shrugged, "I ask a simple question, Miles, was it worth it, the beating, the risk to your life?"

Was it? He had come to avenge a child and had yet to achieve it, nevertheless his journey was not without reward. Miles sidestepped the snakes and took a moment to free his wrists. "I believe so. We must always try, even when failure looms. I have learned a harsh lesson and in the process may have discovered something for the greater good. Only time will tell.

"Then I suggest we make haste, before Guy's men return to finish the job they began or Saladin arrives to harvest his serpents." Thomas sidestepped carefully to avoid the angry snakes. "Dare I ask? Who covets this poison?"

"Who do you think? There is more than one way to win a battle and our enemies employ the most devious of weapons."

"Whereas you...?"

Miles grinned, "I will use whatever comes to hand. I am not without charm when the need arises."

"You and Hugh both."

Miles shrugged his agreement. It was true Hugh was a charmer of women. Jesmina's infatuation as witnessed the previous evening had been proof of that. For himself though, he had yet to meet a woman who could stir his passion beyond the physical act."

"I pity the woman who finds herself bound to you, Miles, you are naught but a whore," scolded Thomas.

"No, Thomas, just loyal to the crown."

"And determined for revenge, it seems."

"With good reason. A whole day is lost. I have yet to deal with Guy and find the boy."

49

Thomas smiled. "I suspect you will be dealing with Guy sooner than you think. I told you, you should have trusted Hugh."

Six

Hugh was waiting when they returned. His renowned patience sorely tested. He paced back and forth, hands clenched tightly behind his back as if he feared, without some measure of self-restraint, he might be compelled to tighten them around his protégé's throat.

"You have news of the boy?" Miles hurled the question at him as he struggled from his horse, anxious not to reveal just how thoroughly he had been beaten.

Hugh took a moment to assess him, head to foot, but seemed less than sympathetic to his injuries. He shook his head with exasperation. "I specifically asked that you stay away from Guy. Which part of my request did you not understand, Miles?"

"The boy was in danger. I had to act."

"I told you I would attend to the boy. Did you not believe me? Did you not think I had the influence to do so, or did you simply *not think*?"

Miles scowled. He was far too old to be scolded like a recalcitrant child. "Perhaps I acted in haste..." he replied begrudgingly. Despite what Hugh might conclude, he wasn't entirely witless. He *had* thought, he had thought of recruiting Thomas into his escapade, but he hadn't thought long enough or hard enough, for if he had, then common sense would have surely prevailed. Nevertheless, he had no intention of admitting that to Hugh.

"Acted in haste? Played directly into Guy's hands..."

"Yes, well..."

"And if it were not for Thomas, I suspect you would have handed victory on a platter to your rival. Do you now see the folly in recklessness, Miles?"

Miles swallowed his humble pie and shook his head. He expected Hugh's disapproval, nay deserved it, but enough was enough. "Not entirely. I have news which may restore your faith in me."

"Indeed?"

"But first, the boy Edmund. Do you have word of him?" Miles waited as Hugh considered his reply.

"The boy is safe for now," he sighed. "No thanks to you. He did indeed run from his master, at your incitement no doubt. Fortunately his flight took him straight into the arms of a trader whose stall was flattened yesterday by Marchant's unruly mob. He is sympathetic to our cause."

"Then all is well?"

"Not entirely. The lad remains the property of his master regardless of where he might hide, and those that provide him with sanctuary do so at great risk. A tangle indeed – and of your own making, Miles. You have placed your rival in an untenable position. He cannot back down. He cannot allow you to make a fool of him in front of his peers. He must respond and we, along with half of Edward's court, await his response with baited breath. You have drawn attention to us all in a most unfortunate manner."

"Guy shall not have him back."

"Then we must seek a way to ensure he has no further claim."

Miles nodded, unsure how Hugh could make that happen but confident in his ability to do so. "Where is the boy, with the Venetians?"

Hugh smiled. "No. He's being cared for in a place where no man may enter. Alas he is too young to appreciate an opportunity missed."

"Jesmina? What madness is this?"

Hugh hushed him with a frown. "Watch your tongue, Miles. I have no wish for my allegiances to be known to all and sundry. The child is currently safer amongst Baybars' women than here with you."

Miles dropped his voice to a hoarse rasp. "And is that who Jesmina really is? Baybars' woman? You play a risky game if that is the case."

"Life itself is a risky game, Miles, and we are all players. Jesmina will care for Edmund until arrangements are made for his return to England."

"He cannot go back to Lincoln. We could not take him. It would be too dangerous for all concerned."

"True, but perhaps he could accompany you when you return to Wildewood. You will have need of a squire on the long journey and perhaps the lad will keep *you* out of trouble."

Miles frowned. His plan to save the boy had not included taking personal responsibility for him. He had business in Northumberland that was better attended to alone. "I am not yet ready to leave."

"You jest, surely. I've seen the look on your face when the trading ships leave port." Hugh's weather beaten face cracked into a broad smile. "Your work here is done, Miles. You are no longer in need of my protection. You have proved your worth, fought bravely for the monarch and picked up more than a trick or two of your own. I can assure you, when this business with Guy is done you'll be more than ready to leave. You'll have Marchant's hounds snapping at your heels until you're clear of The Holy Land, and most likely beyond."

Miles smiled sourly at the thought. He had rattled Guy's cage most soundly and would no doubt suffer the consequences. And, yes, he yearned for his home, the hills and the scent of the deep woods, but he did not relish completing the next stage of his journey, without the comradery and support of his fellow knights.

"We shall all be leaving soon," continued Hugh, as if attuned to his change in mood. "A month here or there is of little concern."

"How can you be so sure, how can you predict the outcome of the campaign?"

Hugh shrugged indifferently. "I know many things. Do not ask me how, it is sufficient that I know and you benefit from my wisdom." He gave a weary sigh and Miles noticed, perhaps for the first time, the age of the man. The last year had taken its toll. Although still handsome, if the interest of the ladies was any measure, his face was now lined and his eyes heavy with fatigue. Miles may have spent a sleepless night with a rope around his neck, but it appeared Hugh had also shunned his bed to further the cause of the child. He was deeply grateful to the man who without fail, always managed to do the right thing, at the appropriate time.

"So, Miles, now we must seek audience with the prince and discover whether all our previous good work for Edward has left a lasting impression."

"You mean to ask for Edward's intervention?"

"I can see no other way. We must broker an arrangement that appeases Guy and leaves the child in your care."

"Would it assist your negotiation to know that Guy's men left me in Saladin's snake pit?"

"Assist in what way?"

"It proves Guy's knowledge of Saladin's trade. Why would he have need of such information if he did not have need of poison?"

Hugh shook his head. "There are many who know of Saladin's expertise, they are not all treasonous."

"But do they all know of the hidden serpent cave? I surely did not until I was thrust amongst them."

"No, I cannot accept Guy's involvement, he has too much to lose over a half-baked poison plot, but nevertheless all knowledge is useful. Leverage is a valuable commodity when negotiations are afoot." He rolled his head from side to side, testing tightened muscles. "Clean yourself up Miles. You cannot attend court looking and smelling like you slept the night with a camel for a bedfellow. You will offend Eleanor and in doing so you will offend Edward and under the circumstances I'm sure you wish to do neither."

Seven

Miles was no stranger to Edward's court. He had attended with Hugh and ridden in the prince's company on numerous forays while on Crusade, but this was the first time that his actions would be the topic of debate and it was important that he achieved the optimum outcome. He was at a disadvantage, unlike Guy he had no wealthy father to sweeten the court and swell the royal coffers, but he did have Hugh and he suspected that Hugh's influence and value was far greater than his enemy appreciated.

"Leave this to me," cautioned Hugh as they entered Edward's chambers. "Hold your tongue and we might yet come away with the boy. Do not give Edward cause to decide in Guy's favour."

Miles nodded. He had every intention of leaving things in Hugh's capable hands. His own attempts to save the boy had been less than successful.

A sluicing in the water trough had rid him of the worst evidence of his beating and his outer garments had been vigourously brushed clean of Acre's dust and debris, all the same, compared to the finery of the royal chambers, he might well have stepped straight from the chaos of battle. He dipped his head in deference and waited for the prince to speak.

"Reynard, I understand you have business to discuss." Edward regarded Miles curiously as he spoke. As if he pondered some issue out-with their current situation and was at pains to recall it fully. Miles shifted uncomfortably.

It would not do for the prince to delve too deeply into his affairs.

"Yes, sire. I am faced with a dilemma that I hope, with your great wisdom, you might ratify."

Edward raised a brow at Hugh's courtly affectation. "And, you..." he gestured with an outstretched hand toward Miles.

"Miles... of Wildewood, sire."

Edward smiled, recognition dawning on a tired face. He waved his attendants away and settled comfortably back against his many cushioned couch. "Ah, yes, I remember you. The reckless young knight who rides at the side of my good friend and advisor, The Fox. I hear good things about you – and I hear bad things. Tell me, Miles, are the tales of your adventures merely exaggeration, designed to curry favour, and woo the ladies, or are you a good and loyal knight who does as he is ordered by his liege – no matter what?"

Miles risked a glance at Hugh. His face was tight with warning. "I am your loyal servant, sire."

"Indeed. How did you find the Mongols?"

Miles blinked, somewhat confused by the question. It had been some time since he and Hugh had made the trek on Edward's behalf to seek the allegiance of the mighty Abagha Khan of il-Khanate.

"Sire, the Mongols are indeed a fearsome race. The journey was most arduous – and dangerous."

"Over seven hundred miles I believe," continued the prince, with some obvious appreciation for the stamina required for such a journey, "and back again in time to deliver the news and join in the attack on Qaqun. You are a man of many talents, Miles. It is unfortunate that the diplomatic negotiations so skilfully administered by your benefactor did not have the desired result."

"The Mongols agreed terms, sire."

"Indeed they did, but they did not deliver when we most desired it, more's the pity. I understand you were wounded at Qaqun. Are your wounds now healed?"

Miles thought of the thigh wound, skilfully attended and sutured by Hugh, and the pain he had suffered as a result of a moment's inattention. The scar remained as a lesson to him but nevertheless he nodded his agreement.

"Good, good. You have served me well, Miles. Long may it continue." He turned his attention back to Hugh and Miles retreated, confused and more than a little wary at Edward's unusual interest in him.

"So tell me, Hugh. How may I repay your undoubted service to the crown?"

"I wish you to intervene in a matter of grave concern, sire."

"Go on."

"A child, a boy who is of great interest to me is currently not well placed. I wish to relocate him to my household."

"Is the child known to me, is he of noble birth, should I be aware of his plight?"

"Nay, sire, he is simply a page, but like the lad here..." he gestured to Miles, "I see potential which shall surely be wasted in his current position."

"Potential, you say." Edward shrugged his confusion."And you cannot arrange this trade yourself. You, the great negotiator cannot agree a price?"

"I'm afraid it is not that simple, sire."

Edward frowned. "Who owns this child?"

"Guy-de-Marchant." Miles suffered Hugh's sudden glare in response to his interruption. He had been told to stay silent, but found he could not and the venom in his words was enough to reveal far more than was wise. A sharp kick at his ankle, reminded him that Hugh, not he, was the man with the prince's ear.

"Ah," was Edward's short reply. He rose from the couch and proceeded to stroll the chamber, seemingly disinterested in the affair as he viewed with obvious contempt the latest gifts presented by the Venetians. When he returned his attention to the men, he focussed solely on Miles, narrowing his eyes shrewdly as he took in the swollen lip and bruised cheek.

"I hear accounts of bad feeling between Marchant and yourself. I see evidence of a recent beating on your face. Tell me, Miles, why do you fight with your fellow knight?" Hugh cleared his throat, pointedly, and was hushed by Edward's raised hand. "Let your protégé speak, Hugh. If you wish my help to extricate this child, I desire to know the origins of the disharmony between the two combatants."

"We do not share the same principles, sire. It is nothing more than that."

Edward shook his head at the obvious understatement. "You will not win my favour by weaving falsehoods."

Miles resisted the urge to glance Hugh's way for support. He was unable to reveal the truth behind his hatred of Guy, as he could not condemn Guy without condemning himself and risking his fellow Templars. The prince believed they followed his orders in Lincoln. Miles could not admit that they had not. Now, too late, he understood the game of political subterfuge played by Hugh and regretted his haste to join in.

The silence in the chamber lengthened until eventually broken by Edward with a measure of irritation in his tone. "I cannot take another man's property without just cause, particularly that belonging to a loyal subject. You give me no cause to intervene. You wish to take a boy into your household? Then I suggest you choose another."

Miles made to step forward, words of demand and denial all but forcing though his tightly closed lips, but Hugh's hand on his arm cautioned him back.

"Sire, I have no wish to sully the name of one of your loyal subjects, but I fear the boy has been mistreated. Why, as we speak he receives treatment for wounds inflicted either by Sir Guy himself, or at his command. His hired men run amok. You are a father, sire. I know you would not wish ill-harm upon a defenceless child." As Edward inclined his head in agreement, Hugh pressed on. "Surely with your good counsel we may find a diplomatic solution to ensure the child's safety."

"William-de-Marchant is a loyal subject and a wealthy man. He supports the crown, and indeed the crusade, in many ways. His son brings seasoned soldiers and an impressive record to the campaign. I will not risk those alliances over the plight of one child..." He paused and turned his attention back to Miles, "Guy...he is your enemy?"

"He is no ally, sire."

"Yet you do not deem it prudent to reveal the reason. Perhaps the child does not mean as much to you as you imagine."

"The child's plight means a great deal to me, sire."

"Then reveal the reason for your disparity."

Miles did not need to glance Hugh's way to feel the warning in his glare. He shifted uncomfortably, looked everywhere but at his mentor and inside, his gut churned. He had to respond if he had any chance of saving the child. "It is a simple disagreement over a woman, sire."

"Ah, I see." Edward smiled, seemingly convinced by the partial truth and Miles let out the breath he'd been holding. "Were I to rule on this matter and free the child into your care, what then? What could I expect in return?"

Miles frowned. The deeds already carried out in Edward's name haunted him daily. They'd made him the tarnished man that he'd become, yet still the prince demanded more. He thought of the child, of his Northumberland home and of an enemy far greater than Guy. He had much yet to achieve, and even more to lose. He could not sacrifice an offer of support from the future king, even though his conscience protested. "You already have my loyalty," he replied humbly "you need only ask for more."

"Then we have a solution." Edward clapped his hands in appreciation of his own brilliance. "The campaign begins to bore me. What use is a truce to a soldier?"

Miles shrugged his confusion.

"We are in need of entertainment are we not?"

"We are?"

"I have in mind a grand spectacle, to remind the heathens of our greatness, our superiority and to show Baybars that we are not bowed by his treaties or his presence on our doorstep. It's time for our brave Christian knights of Acre to demonstrate their prowess via a tournament."

"A tournament?" Miles lips twitched. The thought of combat with Guy was more than a little tempting.

"Indeed. A chance for you and your rival to settle your differences in a noble way."

"And what of the child, sire?"

"You want the child? Then you may fight for him, you and Guy. The victor takes the child."

"And the loser?" asked Hugh, his tone betraying his reservations at the prince's solution.

Edward smiled slyly. "Do you intend to lose, Miles?"

"No, sire."

"Then you have no need to worry about a forfeit."

"Finally I get to deal soundly with Guy," said Miles as they hurried back to camp. He could not hide his satisfaction, in fact he could not have asked for more, a chance to rid himself of an enemy, with any outcome protected by a royal sanction.

Hugh did not share his enthusiasm. "That supposes you have the skill to win."

"You trained me, Hugh. You know I can beat him."

"And what then?"

"What do you mean? I win, I save the boy."

"And Guy? Kill him and you make an enemy of one of the most powerful men in England."

"William-de-Marchant is an old man, I do not fear him."

"You should. He is a man who values his offspring above all else. If harm comes to his heir, then harm will surely follow the killer."

"What do you suggest?"

"I have no answer. If you kill him, you become a marked man, despite the royal sanction. If you spare his life, you shame the man and he will make it his business to repay you."

"But the boy will be safe."

Hugh smiled wearily, "Yes, the boy will be safe."

"Then all will be well."

"I very much doubt that, Miles, for in addition to exacerbating the issue of Guy, you have now attracted one more."

"And what is that?"

"You now owe our future king a further favour. And as we know to our cost that is not a good position to be in."

Miles thought back to Lincoln and the last favour they had carried out for the prince. He nodded slowly. Hugh was correct. They carried a heavy enough load without adding more, but there was little to be done about it now.

Eight

Edward was correct. Acre was indeed in need of entertainment. Extended conflict had wrung the life from the stronghold and left it war weary and rife with inter-racial squabbling and suspicion. What better way to unite the people, if only for a day. Word of the joust spread quickly and Christians, Muslims, Venetian merchants and even the great sea traders who docked in the port, packed the arena to watch the spectacle. Between the fine robes of Acre's wealthy, peeked urchins and beggars, while up high, away from the common folk, in a hastily constructed pavilion, sat Edward and Eleanor surrounded by their attendants and favoured guests.

The stronghold heaved with knights keen to show off their prowess and prove themselves both in the tilt and in hand to hand combat. It mattered naught that the sport was as dangerous as open warfare and that they were as likely to meet their maker to the cheers of a rambunctious audience, as they were fighting Mamluks in the desert. For the men who took part, it was an important opportunity to demonstrate their skill and courage not only to a most appreciative audience but to their enemies as well. In an effort to protect the lives of as many of his English knights as possible, Edward decreed that every lance be capped, but even so each man entered at considerable risk of serious injury or even death.

Around the main arena, traders squeezed stalls into the smallest space, anxious to capitalize on the captive audience. The air was pungent with the combatant aromas of spices and sweet and savoury delicacies and for once there was an air of jubilance about the place. The bawdy ruckus of testosterone drenched men preparing for battle was contrasted by music performed by the various troubadours and minstrels who entertained for the crowds ahead of the official opening. Acrobats tumbled, thrown high into the air by their counterparts, their brightly coloured garb dazzling in the sun. Dwarves, barely the size of children, juggled balls and flaming torches, and in the centre of the arena two men struggled to restrain a frantic, chained bear as snarling dogs, crazed by the din, strained at the ends of their tethers.

In the shadows beneath the timber framed pavilion, Miles rested his forehead against the flank of his horse and took a moment to shut out the madness. He closed his eyes and drew a long steadying breath. He was ready, focused, motivated to succeed, and confident in his ability to do so. And yet, a small voice in his head whispered caution. Guy, a man who rose each day in the certain knowledge that all endeavours were weighed in his favour, had agreed far too readily to the combat. A competition, witnessed by so many and officiated by the royal couple, was surely beyond corruption even by one so gifted at the art. Miles ignored the warning thrumming gently inside. Whatever trickery Guy may think to employ, he was ready for it. He was not afraid; indeed he looked forward to meeting Guy with certain relish.

That did not mean he was without concern, but what caused his gut to churn and his skin to prickle with apprehension, was not the ordeal to be faced in the arena, but his promise to the prince. He had vowed his loyalty to the crown with absolute honesty - but he knew with certainty that he could not do Edward's private bidding again and survive with his integrity intact.

"Miles, the tournament begins. Are you prepared?" Thomas emerged from the shadows, concern etched on his face as Miles' introspective expression suggested that he was anything but ready.

Miles turned, his face creasing immediately into a genuine grin for his good friend. "Thomas, you should know by now, I am always ready for a fight."

"Good. Then, come and watch. There is mayhem in the arena. The bear, poor beast, is making a bid for freedom and the dogs have scattered the dwarves like so many skittles. The crowd are most appreciative of the additional entertainment."

"And Hugh, where is he? I anticipated a lecture."

"He sits alongside the royal party. To ensure fair play, I wager. Guy is a scoundrel. It would not surprise me if he uses his influence to corrupt the outcome."

Miles shrugged beneath his heavy armour. "I expect he will try, he would not be the man we know if he did not, but I believe Edward seeks a greater prize and will not take kindly to Guy's interference."

"A greater prize?"

"Don't ask. I have no answer for you - not yet at least."

Reaching out, Thomas placed a hand on Miles' arm between the armoured plates and roughly squeezed his encouragement.

"You are a good man, Miles. Headstrong and impulsive, perhaps, and yes you have erred in the past, as we all have, but regardless, you are good man. Whatever happens, now or in the future, do not forget that. You can triumph over Guy. You *will* triumph over Guy. You are stronger. You have right on your side. Just remember everything you have been taught and remember *everything* he has done."

As he rode out into the arena Miles ignored the cheers of the crowds, the dazzling colours and the heat of the sun, instead he turned his attention to the royal pavilion and scanned the dais for his benefactor. His armour, his horse, the skill with which he wielded his sword, indeed his very life, he owed it all to Hugh. He accepted that today's contest was as much about proving his worth to his mentor as it was about saving a child and vanquishing a rival. Relief rippled through him as he located Hugh standing behind the prince. The man dipped his head briefly in acknowledgement and with that simple gesture Miles let out the breath he'd been holding.

He shifted his gaze back to the arena. The bear had been recaptured. Shackled, and confined to a cage, to be tormented afresh another day. It swung its head back and forth, its tongue lolled from the side of its open, toothless jaw. A pathetic prisoner with no hope of reprieve, Miles watched as it was trundled past on a cart. He felt its pain.

"The beast needs water," he muttered to the oafs who pulled the cart, but his words were lost amid the noise, and the bear and its handlers were soon gone. The remaining entertainers were corralled at the entrance, squeezed behind or sat atop the gaily coloured barriers, hands clapping, heels kicking at the painted heraldic symbols. They cheered at him as he past, but he had no room in his head for civility. As he entered the main body of the arena, drummers pounded a beat that excited the remainder of the crowd into a frenzied cacophony of delirium.

Inside the heavy armour, sweat coated Miles' skin, beading on his forehead. Rivulets found the path of least obstruction and chased a course through the wire of his short stubble. His heart pounded, his chest heaved for air within the constraints of mail and metal. His breath misted on the metal chin guard, each new inhalation bringing with it the remembered taste of battle and death. Beneath him the leather saddle creaked reassuringly as the horse trembled and skittered with nervous energy. Its ears flicked back and forth as it awaited Miles' command.

Across the arena Guy also waited. Edward raised a gloved hand. The drumming stopped. The crowd fell silent and Miles dropped his visor.

The first blow, when it came, took Miles by surprise. Thundering toward each other, they had made two passes without contact. Guy's lance was naturally aimed to knock him clean from the saddle and break a few bones on the way. Miles expected no less and had every intention to make his own lance work for him first, by ensuring that it was Guy who was unseated. However when his horse stumbled at the last moment, on a discarded juggling ball, his lance missed it's mark and instead of connecting against Guy's shield, he felt the full force of Guy's lance rip through his armoured shoulder plate tearing the flesh below. Miles crumpled over his horse's neck, clinging desperately to his own lance as Guy galloped past, roaring his superiority. Remnants of Miles' armour plate impaled and held high, were proof enough that Guy's lance was uncapped. The crowd roared their disapproval, Edward leapt to his feet, and Guy was forced to forgo the lance and meet Miles on the next run without it, or suffer the wrath of the mob and the displeasure of the prince.

"Hold fast, Miles," yelled Thomas as Miles turned his horse for the return charge and almost toppled from the saddle. The weighty lance slipped from his grasp, his shoulder shrieked with pain, but he could not give up. He must unseat his opponent if he wanted to save the boy. All around the crowd began to chant, their words unintelligible, their fervour unchecked. "They shout for you, Miles. Take heart."

Miles nodded. He thought again of the boy, the reason he was there, and then his focus switched to Guy and bile rose into his throat. He swapped his reins into his left hand, freeing his uninjured arm to hold a weapon. Blood leached from his wound soaking his sleeve and gloves. The reins were slippy in his grasp. Thomas handed him a length of chain. "You know what you must do, Miles. Unseat him and the boy is yours."

"I ... I will. This time I will." His vision blurred. The racket from the crowd intensified. He stooped a little lower over the horse's neck.

"Miles!"

The sting of Thomas' urgent tone jerked him upright.

"Use the pain to focus. You have the advantage. Guy believes you are beaten. He becomes lazy and lacks attention. You know what to do, aim for his wrist and you will disable the hand that wields the sword, or dodge the sword and aim for his head, and you will surely unseat him."

Miles shuddered. His left arm began to tremble involuntarily and the reins slipped from his grasp. He knew the dangers of excessive blood loss, he had to act swiftly before he was totally incapacitated, but rather than sharpening his focus the pain merely confused him and his movements became even more sluggish.

"Here, chew on this." Thomas reached up, lifted Miles' visor and pushed a wodge of berry pulp between his lips. "Chew but do not swallow, the pain will abate in a moment." He gathered up the fallen reins and knotted them loosely around the pommel. Use your knees and your weight as you have been trained to do, the horse will do the rest. Do not fall, Miles. The boy is depending on you."

This time when the horse began the charge, there was no accompanying pain, merely a cloying, heady, warmth that rolled up his body and cocooned him. Miles felt none of the jarring hoof beats, or the rolling motion that slid each armoured section seamlessly against the other. He heard none of the din from the crowd, the screams of encouragement or the verbalised bloodlust. In place of Guy's scornful face he saw the image of a boy with a bow, earnest and trusting. Instead of pain, he felt the soft caress of his mother's smile, but in direct contrast to this instant euphoria, his ears were filled with a sound that had haunted his dreams since Lincoln – a young woman's screams of terror. As they reached their horrific pinnacle,

68

he swung the chain and launched it directly at his enemy's head.

The chain wrapped around Guy's helmet, snapped his head back sharply and his body followed, lifted clean out of the saddle. He hit the ground like a felled beast, his limbs askew, his face guard wrenched open. All around the spectators yelled their approval, stamping their feet in solidarity. It seemed that Guy's infamy had preceded him.

Miles grabbed the reins and yanked his horse to a juddering halt. The beast heaved a laboured breath and he matched it with one of his own. He swayed, precariously, a combination of blood loss and opiate, and then he lifted his visor, drew his sword and approached Guy's prone body, guiding his horse around the dividing barrier.

On the ground, Guy stirred. His limbs jerked as if he were in the final throes and death courted him, but as Miles leaned over him from the horse's back, Guy's eyes shot open. The look on his face was one of unadulterated hatred.

"You have lost and I have won," stated Miles coldly. "That is it. Over." He spat out the berry pulp and wiped away the juice with the back of his glove.

"This will never be over." Guy's words bubbled from his twisted mouth, blood foamed between his lips and with an incredible effort he hauled himself up on one elbow and vomited the foulness onto the sand.

"The boy is now mine, whether that pleases you or not. The prince has decreed it. There is nothing more to say on the matter." Miles paused as a spasm of pain left him breathless. "Gather your harbingers and be gone from Acre by sunset, or you can be assured that I will finish what has been started here, with a sword to your belly." He pulled the horse away and turned toward the pavilion. As he approached, to the deafening cheers of the crowd, he caught Edward's shrewd smile and if his mind had been clear he might have wondered at the game he had just been party to and who the true victor was.

69

Edward raised his hand and the crowd fell silent once more. "Well fought, Miles, bloodied but victorious nevertheless. Once again you prove your tenacity and determination to win at all costs. I have many uses for a man with those skills."

He had not room in his muddled brain for the meaning behind the prince's words. It was sufficient that he understood the nuance'. He would never be totally free from his past, certainly not here in The Holy Land.

Blood seeped from Miles' wound. His Templar tabard was drenched with it, the edges of the cross blurred, just as he was. With no more berries to numb the effects, pain returned with a vengeance. He raised his head and sought out Hugh.

Hugh rushed to the lower edge of the pavilion, pushing aside the spectators who reached out over the rail to lay a hand on the new champion of Acre. His face creased with concern as he took a swift inventory of Miles' condition. Despite the severity of the wound, he could not hide his pride – and relief at the outcome of the combat.

"Miles! Miles, a good result." He punched the air and those around him echoed his satisfaction.

Miles turned his head. In the centre of the arena Guy's attendants fussed about the man. He was on his feet, albeit with a man on either side lending support, but on his feet nevertheless and besides the wound to his head, he was unmarked by the fall. A broken bone, a scar to mar his fine features, but that was all. Was it a good result? He was no longer sure.

"I shall savour it later," he slurred as pain blurred his vision once more.

"Savour it now," declared Hugh with a smile. "You are a champion in the eyes of Acre, let the people see why you risk your life and they will applaud you all the more... *and protect you in your need*," he added under his breath. He reached behind and yanked a small boy from the shadows into the light and held him aloft. The crowd hushed as

Hugh extended his arms and dangled the child beyond the edge of the pavilion.

"Meet your protector, Edmund," said Hugh, but as the child squirmed in his hands Hugh was pulled off-balance and the boy, wide-eyed and fearful slipped from his grasp and tumbled free.

Miles watched him fall as if in a dream, slowly, his thin arms flapping – not wildly as in real time, but with the grace of a bird that soars high on the desert thermals. His overlarge clothes billowed, his feet pedalled and his mouth formed a silent scream. When it seemed the fall would continue forever, Miles was pulled from his stupor by Hugh's insistent cry.

"Miles!"

The spectators were unified in a horrified guilty gasp both appalled and entertained by the sudden threat to the child, and in response Miles drew a frantic breath and kicked his startled horse closer. He shot out his good arm as the boy tumbled past. His fingers, grasped wildly at the soiled velveteen jerkin, sliding the length of it before finally gaining a hold, but to no avail, the undernourished child slipped out of the overlarge garment and continued to fall, his head mere feet from the ground before Miles leaning low from the saddle, extended his reach and yanked him to the safety of his lap.

The crowd roared their appreciation and in the midst of the mayhem Miles closed his eyes and prayed. God had seen fit to watch over them both. Miles asked that He be merciful for just a little longer. His shoulder bled afresh, his nerve endings screamed at him for mercy and his entire body shuddered with adrenalin and shock. He reopened his eyes and turned to the boy.

"Edmund, it seems I am very much in need of a boy to assist me from my horse." He smiled wearily, "Are you such a boy?"

Edmund's lip trembled, his words diluted by tears, as he struggled to comprehend the turn of events. "Aye, my lord...I am that boy."

"Good. Then, my little archer, learn your craft well, for we have a long and arduous journey ahead of us and, I wager, many obstacles in our way."

"Where do we travel, my lord?" the boy asked, his eyes wide with wonder.

"Home, Edmund. All the way home to Wildewood."

*****

Assassin's Curse

Novella Two

The Crusader stronghold of Acre: 1272 A.D.

A lone assassin threatens the life of Prince Edward. Only one man can save the future king from certain death, but in doing so Hugh-de-Reynard risks execution as a heretic. As royal birthday celebrations lower the state of alert, Jesmina, the sultry daughter of Saladin the Snake Master, courts the attentions of Acre's good and evil and Miles uncovers a plot by rival knights. It falls to Jesmina to save the day. But can she be trusted?

One

The gates opened at dawn and by mid-afternoon the steady stream of travellers determined to enter Acre had not abated. Arriving by horse, camel, and overloaded ramshackle carts they channelled through the narrow thoroughfare in a ragged heaving procession. Those without the benefit of wheeled or four-legged transportation were on foot, head down, shoulders hunched with the weight of the goods and chattels strapped to their back. Nanny goats heavy with milk were tugged along at the end of rough twine while bud-horned kids struggled to keep up. Bleating frantically, the infants risked separation from their mother's pendulous udder. Tender young goat meat, roasted gently over a hot flame was a welcome addition to any feast. Its provenance rarely questioned by an empty belly.

No matter the length of journey or method of transport, all new arrivals appeared weary and thankful to have reached their destination before the gates were closed. A subtle excitement flickered through the crowd, gathering momentum. Sparked by anticipation of the spectacle to come it manifested itself in random, undisciplined displays of pushing, shoving and more volatile disagreements over trifling matters. The land beyond the city walls may well have been fraught with danger, but even the crusader stronghold was not without risk.

Amid the hustle and bustle children darted, small practised hands slipped beneath the robes of the unwary, and those with a purse worth taking were relieved of it before they'd taken more than a dozen steps inside the city. Despite the raucous racket of bellowing beasts and crying infants, the occasional shout of an injured party could be heard, but the crowd was far too tightly packed to allow for pursuit. The beggars, cross-legged in narrow doorways, gave slack-jawed toothless grins. The urchin thieves mocked in high-pitched feral whoops, and beleaguered merchants held up their hands in dismay.

Miles of Wildewood steadied his mount against the human tide and attempted to concentrate on the task at hand. More at home on the battlefield, he viewed the crowd with a long-suffering sigh. It was impossible to control such a mass effectively and yet that was what he and his fellow knights had been instructed to do.

Hugh-de-Reynard, strategist and royal confidante' was unconvinced at the sense behind the Prince's latest plan to celebrate the royal birthday with yet another lavish spectacle. The previous tournament, instrumental in delivering young Edmund into Miles' care, was barely a month past and Miles' resulting wound not yet fully healed, but the success of the event had done much to improve Edward's mood. The prince might be on the cusp of abandoning his campaign and returning to England but he had no intention of departing Acre without leaving a lasting impression. The open invitation however, was less to do with princely benevolence and more a subtle plan to taunt the continual thorn in his side, Sultan Baybars. As far as Hugh was concerned it was a huge misjudgement on Edward's part. Amid the teeming throng, beneath the guise of peasant, beggar or desert prince, Edward's enemies had been given an incredible opportunity to gain access to their quarry.

A sharp whistle cut through the din and drew Miles' attention to a tall building directly opposite. He shaded his eyes with one hand and scanned the crumbling stonework. Thomas Blackmore was positioned on the flat roof. Concealed as he was within the shadows it took a moment for Miles to locate him. He gestured urgently and Miles followed his direction to a mounted, hooded figure who sought anonymity by keeping to the outer edge of the rabble. The mount was not the heavy destrier favoured by the Templars, but a handsome Arabian stallion with a finely chiselled, intelligent head. Its milk-white coat was dappled with tracery as delicate as a spider-web. It pranced and skittered sideways into the crowd, drawing indignant curses and covetous glances in equal measure from those forced aside.

Indeed, Miles himself was caught by the sheer beauty of the beast, as it tossed its mane and whinnied angrily. A remarkable animal, it commanded attention with its unquestionable provenance. The property of a rich man, of that there was no doubt. His gaze lingered as he found himself estimating the value and calculating his own worth.

Thomas gave another insistent whistle. "Miles! Pay attention, for pity's sake. You're not here to admire horse flesh...or flesh of any kind for that matter." The gruff reminder shook Miles from his day-dream. Thomas gesticulated impatiently, drawing a gloved hand across his own throat to emphasize his concern at both horse and rider.

After four hours of mind-numbing sentry duty, relieved only by the occasional need to intervene in petty merchant squabbles, Miles was weary of Thomas' over-caution. The man was seeing threats where there were none. Overweight, bug-eyed carpet-traders, skinny goat-herders, even a one-legged Bedouin astride his spitting camel had initiated the same response. Miles suspected he was the butt of a game. The rules of the jest determined over a flagon or two by Thomas and the other men to repay him for some prior misdeed. Or, as was more likely, by Hugh as he endeavoured to glean the last ounce of duty from his protégé' before the long awaited departure from Acre.

"Miles! Make haste." Now, Thomas' bellow could clearly be heard above the racket and the knight left his post in the shadows and ran toward the edge of the roof as if he meant to leap from it. Alarmed at this sudden escalation of concern, Miles swung his attention back to the object of Thomas' scrutiny. The hooded rider, alerted by the very same warning, yanked the stallion to one side, took a short whip to its flank, and forced the beast through the scattering crowd, seeking cover behind a pair of camels before disappearing down a narrow alley. Thomas skidded to a halt inches from the roof-edge, wind-milled his arms desperately to regain balance before altering course and making off across the roof-tops in pursuit.

Miles cursed aloud. Game or not, he had no option but to give chase. He had no desire to spend the heat of the day negotiating Acre's maze of twisted alleyways, at Thomas' dubious direction, but the lure of a closer look at the milk-white stallion decided him, and his own horse took only the slightest encouragement to stretch its legs.

He caught up with the stallion by sheer good luck for the beast was far nimbler than his own. As the tangled labyrinth and the hooded rider's questionable sense of direction combined, the stallion faltered and Miles took advantage. Squeezed flank to flank they dodged the detritus of Acre's merchant quarter, the earthenware pots piled high, the freshly dyed fabrics hung like pennants to dry in the sun, the squawking fowl and barking dogs, until forced by the momentum of the chase they barged through the tanner's yard splashing and skidding hock-deep in the stinking piss. Miles gagged, holding desperately to the contents of his stomach as he urged his horse on and out the other side. As the cluttered street narrowed again he took his chance and launched himself at his quarry. He caught the rider unawares with a sweeping blow which knocked them both from the saddle, while momentum and Miles' full weight slammed them both to the baked earth.

Despite his fall being cushioned by his captive, the percussion of the impact jarred throughout him and his recent shoulder injury protested cruelly. He ignored the pain, grabbed his wriggling prisoner by the throat and ripped back the hood.

Sultry eyes flashed angrily beneath sooty lashes. Full lips twitched into a haughty smile and Miles shook his head in confusion.

"Jesmina!"

Snake trader's daughter, sultan's woman, and Hugh's mysterious lady friend – she was certainly a mistress of many roles. But what was she doing riding into Acre unaccompanied? Miles doubted that she'd been extended a personal invitation.

"I see your humours are fully restored, Miles, a shame indeed that your manners fail you. Is this the way you treat a lady?" Her breathless pant softened the barbed words.

He removed his hand from her throat, but was deliberately slow to release her from beneath him. He found himself not only seduced by the magnificent horse, but tempted by its rider. She awaited his response with an arched brow. His own lips twitched with ill-concealed amusement as he imagined Hugh's reaction to her arrival. He would be sure to deliver the news in person.

When propriety, and the imminent arrival of Thomas, demanded a more chivalrous handling of his voluptuous captive he eased himself up and reaching out a hand, pulled her to her feet.

"Pardon, my lady. I trust you are not injured." He dipped his head apologetically, a little late perhaps, considering he had almost pummelled her into the sand. "This....," he swept a hand at her attempt at disguise, "is most confusing. Had I known it was you I would have reacted more appropriately. May I ask what brings you to Acre, cloaked and unaccompanied, and why you flee from an honourable Templar, like a common thief?"

"Honourable? Phsst" she made the disparaging hiss through her teeth, yanked her hand from his and proceeded to brush the dust from her clothes impatiently. "You may ask, Miles of Wildewood, though I do not intend to favour you with an answer." Her red painted lips slid into a sly smile and Miles stepped back to study her. Yet another who thought to play games at his expense. He flexed his shoulder painfully and considered how best to deal with her. He could not allow her presence to compromise Hugh's position.

"If you wish to continue your journey then you must answer, and answer promptly, before we are surrounded by over-eager militia, whom I can assure you, are far less chivalrous than I." He tried to maintain a stern demeanour, but his mirth at the situation betrayed him. "It has been a long morning and my fellow Templars are starved of action, who knows how they will respond when confronted by such an alluring spy."

"Spy? I think not."

"Then why so coy? Reveal the nature of your covert business. Do you seek Hugh or another? Do you carry a message from your father? If so you may entrust the matter to me, I will ensure it reaches its rightful recipient."

Jesmina shrugged noncommittally as if she underestimated the risk of her actions and doubted Miles' authority to restrain her.

"Jesmina, take heed. This is not the time for games. It is clearly not safe for you in Acre. Your connection to the sultan carries with it no small amount of mistrust."

"My connection? And how do you suppose, I, a mere snake-trader's daughter, am connected to one with such power?"

Miles faltered, his knowledge was based purely on hear-say and the bawdy imaginings of drunken men. Jesmina's relationship with the sultan was the subject of many campfire discussions, none of which he felt prudent to divulge.

Laughing softly at his discomfort, Jesmina wagged a scolding finger. "Miles, your eyes betray your thoughts, be sure to avert your gaze in Hugh's presence or you shall have his displeasure to deal with as well as mine. In any case, do you suppose the sultan has no men to do his bidding? That he relies upon women to fight his cause? Do you suspect I carry a weapon concealed about my person, in the folds of my cloak, or between my breasts?" Miles gaze dropped to her ample cleavage. He knew all too well where she stowed her secrets. "You may search if you wish," she continued slyly. "But I can assure you, I carry naught but information for our mutual friend."

Miles sighed. There lay his next problem – Hugh. His benefactor would not take kindly to the fact that, despite her questionable reputation, Jesmina had been chased like a common thief through the streets of Acre. She had after all, been most helpful in the past, to both Hugh and himself. He cast a quick eye to the roofline, Thomas would soon be upon them and he did not intend to be drawn further into the entanglement by his friend's questions.

"Hugh is expecting you?" he asked eventually.

"He will welcome me with open arms when he hears what I have to say."

"I don't doubt it." Miles was not convinced. Hugh's position was delicate enough without his private allegiances being made public. Although no one would fail to appreciate his choice in women, Jesmina was after all quite beautiful, those who sought to blacken his name would make much of her connection to Sultan Baybars. Miles turned away, he couldn't think clearly in her presence. Perhaps the fall had addled his brain.

He whistled softly to his horse. The animal was trained to stop and stand fast should he fall in battle. It stood by him now, silent and resolute. He reached out and idly patted its shoulder, a welcome distraction. "Who knows that you visit Acre?" he asked as he gathered up the reins.

"No one?"

"No one. Are you certain?"

"As certain as one can be in this land of spies and whisperers. Deceit stalks the shadows, as you are well aware."

Miles resisted the urge to look over his shoulder. Was anyone really as they appeared? He stepped away from her and turned his attention to the stallion. Corralled at the end of the alley, nostrils flaring, flanks quivering with nervous energy, it was primed and ready for further flight. Its cobweb markings fluttering like so many butterflies. Miles would have given almost anything to own such an animal. Now that it was close at hand he could see that it was indeed a product of the sultan's breeding stock and wondered what Jesmina had forfeited in exchange for the beast. He approached carefully, hand outstretched. "Shush now..." he murmured. The stallion's belligerent snort was answered by the calming wicker of his own horse, and when his hand brushed the stallion's neck the animal bowed its head submissively.

"Ah, I see you are a charmer of horses *and* women."

Miles shrugged. "Both skills have uses, but now is not the time to elaborate on either. You must make haste Jesmina. If you will not entrust me with your message then I shall bring Hugh to you, but you cannot dally here in Acre's gutter nor can you be seen abroad with the courtiers. You bring risk to all who know of your association."

"My association?"

"You court the good and the bad, the advisors and decision makers. You arrive astride the sultan's most magnificent horse, naturally there are those who will assume you also come at his bidding."

"Do you...assume?"

Miles sighed. In truth he didn't have the answer. He recalled his first meeting with the snake-trader's daughter and the attraction that sparked between her and Hugh. Certainly she was a temptress. Undoubtedly she could turn a man's head and distract him from his duty. But he knew that Hugh was not a man to be easily corrupted. Hugh trusted Jesmina. Therefore he must trust her also.

He relaxed his stance and smiled. "I have not yet thanked you for caring for young Edmund and shielding him from my enemy Guy-de-Marchant. The man is a devil. The boy was in great danger. I am in your debt."

"So you are, Miles, and I shall be sure to hold you to it." Jesmina took the reins from Miles, her fingers lingering unnecessarily within his. Miles shook his head at her obvious mischief, and helped her mount. When she was safely seated, she tucked her hair beneath her hood and smiled. "The boy is fortunate to have you as his protector. Is he well?"

"Indeed, he strives to please."

Her soft laughter raised the hairs on the back of his neck. But for Hugh, he would certainly have taken their association further.

"Ahh to please," she purred "my sole aim in life..."

Miles doubted the truth of that, but all the same he returned her smile. "Then, my lady, do me the honour of pleasing me. Take your fine stallion and be gone before the militia come upon us and I am forced to behave in a less than chivalrous manner. Be at the eastern gate as the bell is sounded for curfew. Hugh shall meet you there."

Jesmina shook her head. "I cannot wait that long. My news is most urgent."

"If it is, then you'd do well to confide in me now."

"My information is for Hugh's ears only."

"Yet, as you know, I act in his stead. Do you not trust me, Jesmina?"

Indecision wrinkled Jesmina's brow. It appeared they were both afflicted by caution and suspicion. Nevertheless curiosity teased as Miles wondered what it was that she deemed so important. "You can tell me," he coaxed.

"Alas I cannot. I shall await Sir Hugh in the shadow of the church of St John."

"You would be safer inside, mademoiselle."

"I think not. You may be welcome at Knights Hall, but I suspect I shall not. As you say, my assumed associations light the pyre of fear."

Miles grimaced. The Templars and Hospitallers had many differences. As a result he was no more welcome at Knights Hall than she. "Perhaps you're right."

She smiled, dipping her head in acknowledgement of his begrudging admission. "I shall take refreshment with the Persians and rest by the spice trader's stall. Bring Hugh to me before the celebrations begin, or I will have no option but to seek him out."

"You must allow me something, Jesmina, a word or token. Hugh will not take leave of his duties at the mere promise of a raised veil."

She leaned down and teased her lips against his cheek. Her whisper was hot against his skin. "Then tell him my father is inordinately busy today."

Two

Thomas dropped heavily to the ground, scattering broken tiles at his feet and Miles' horse took a startled step back. The rapid chase across the many levels of Acre's roof-tops had taken its toll. Perspiration coated Thomas' face. Exasperation coloured his words. He braced his hands against his thighs and heaved in a ragged breath. "You allowed him to slip through your fingers?"

Miles shrugged. "So it would seem." He shot a quick cautious glance toward the end of the alley but Jesmina was gone. A flash of golden mane, a ripple of cobwebbed flank, and she had slipped between the flapping sheets of drying cloth, subsumed back into the chaos of Acre as if their meeting had simply been imagination on his part. He gathered up his reins and calmed his horse.

Thomas' brow furrowed with confusion. "Too much ale or too much sun?"

"Neither. It appears you, not I, are the one bent double with exertion."

"Well there has to be a good reason why the great Miles of Wildewood fails to capture his quarry. I suggest you are not fully recovered, my friend. Or perhaps you have better things to do?" Thomas stepped close and narrowed his eyes suspiciously.

"I wager we all have better things to do, Thomas, yet Hugh demands that we spend our days counting camels rather than defending The Cross."

"True, this is a pox of a job. While we play sentry our good *friends* The Hospitallers have caught themselves a desert rat and have assured the gratitude of the prince." Thomas snorted his rancour at being outsmarted by the rival knights.

Miles leaned in, any mention of The Knights of St John, served to pique his curiosity. "Indeed? Tell me more."

"A rancid, thieving scoundrel who just yesterday we would have happily put a sword through, has declared his wish to exchange one God for another and Edward, and by proxy His Eminence the Pope, are delighted."

Miles frowned. "Does the heathen seek to abandon the prophet to escape the bite of the blade?"

"Miles, you are ever the sceptic."

"With good cause."

"Nay, the man is not a prisoner. He presented at the gate with the other pilgrims, pleading epiphanies and Lord knows what. It's a miracle...apparently." Thomas made a swift sign of the cross on his chest.

"It'll be a miracle if it's anything but trickery," muttered Miles. "This whole thing is madness. Hugh sees Mamluk shadows at every juncture, though I wager they are merely Hospitaller creations. And while they sit back and laugh, we run about wielding torches into the darkness."

Miles walked his horse as they made their way back onto the main thoroughfare. Although distracted by the latest Hospitaller intrigue, his mind was filled with Jesmina and her cryptic message. If as he suspected, Hugh's ongoing investigations into the poisoning at St George-de-Lebeyre were about to conclude, then a number of influential people would be seeking to protect themselves from accusation. Hugh, or indeed the prince himself, could be at risk and the gates of the city should be closed with no more admitted, whether they be pilgrims or princes. Then again, he was not convinced at Jesmina's true purpose. As with the rival knights, she played a fickle game. Had she wished to avert disaster, she need only have relayed her message in full. No doubt there was more to her sudden arrival than first appeared. Why else had she run from him? To draw him into a trap perhaps? Or simply to distract him from something more important?

He glanced quickly at the buildings which narrowed in around them and imagined enemies poised at every darkened window. Flesh and blood enemies he could deal with, indeed he would relish the distraction, anything to relieve the boredom of a truce. But he sensed the current threat hanging over their heads would not be banished by a sharp blade.

"Baybars could have a hundred men within these walls and we'd be none the wiser," he muttered sourly. "The sooner this day, indeed this campaign is over and we are all bound for England, the happier I will be."

Thomas nodded his agreement. The Templars were restless, all keen to return to their own lands with the trophies and wealth they'd accrued during crusade. Acre's commerce had lined their pockets while their valour on the battlefield had not gone without its own reward.

"Where is he?" asked Miles.

"Whom?"

"He who alleges allegiance to The Cross."

"Edward demanded his presence. He wishes to make the most of the situation. I suspect he intends to taunt the sultan and make a spectacle of the man at this evening's entertainment. The Saracen may believe he will be taking holy orders, yet instead I wager he'll be rubbing shoulders with jesters and baited bears."

"And Hugh, what does he make of this?"

Thomas shook his head. "Hugh is elsewhere. I imagine he has missed the excitement. It was only by chance that I heard the news myself. The St Johns' are bragging, and those with any sense are listening while pretending not to hear."

"Where?"

"They gather by the arena. Black cloaked harpies full of their own importance. The spectators are crammed like pigeons in a pie, a captive audience for their boasts."

"A pox on the Hospitallers. It is Hugh's whereabouts that concerns me most. What steals his attention from such an event? Boast or not, I wager he'd have interest in any desert dweller who wheedles his way into the royal court."

"Diplomacy, peace-making, security, call it what you will," said Thomas with a shrug. "Hugh meets with many. Why do you think he keeps us busy? He prepares for our departure and makes deals with those who would prefer us gone with naught but horse and armour. I fear he has some difficult negotiations ahead."

Miles snorted. Hugh was a master at negotiation. "Then I regret I must leave you to count camels alone, Thomas. I must speak with Hugh and I wager the lad will know of his whereabouts. Edmund has his ear to the ground and his snout to the four winds, a skill of great value when all around engage in subterfuge."

"Subterfuge? What do you know?" Thomas stood aside as Miles mounted his horse.

"Naught of value."

"I know you, Miles. I can tell by the look in your eyes...and the ochre smudged across your cheek. You know something. Do not think to avert disaster by yourself. You have proven time and time again that your reckless actions have unwelcome consequences for all."

Miles faltered. The less who knew of Jesmina's arrival the better for all, but Thomas was correct. He should not act alone, particularly where the prince's safety was concerned.

"I simply carry a message for Hugh. Whether it is the fanciful yearnings of a wanton woman or a matter of dire consequence, is questionable. Either way I must deliver it."

Thomas sighed. "A woman. There's always a woman. Our lives would be so much simpler without them."

Miles grinned. "And so much less enjoyable, but I need not tell *you* that, Thomas."

Thomas studied him in silence for a moment, as if he doubted the simplicity of Miles' account and awaited further clarification. When none was forthcoming he merely shrugged. "Then, as you say, the lad will know where to find Hugh. Though I fear his attention has been distracted of late. The boy has been making a nuisance of himself around the entertainer's camp. The Great and Wondrous Maleficius should be paying you for his time."

"Maleficius?"

"The animal trainer. They say he is an enchanter, a magician."

"A magician, then perhaps he can cast a spell and help me find Hugh."

"Miles, guard your tongue." Thomas crossed himself again, and cast an anxious eye to the heavens. "Is your message so urgent, it cannot wait until curfew? Hugh will be bound to appear alongside the prince."

"I believe so."

"Yet clearly you're not convinced, or you'd not be wasting time debating the virtues of the Hospitallers. Share your concern and I will help you decide?"

"Who knows the depths of Hugh's entanglements, who am I to judge which is significant and which is not. Perhaps this will wait until he returns, perhaps not."

"Enough of your riddles, Miles. Is there something I can do to assist that does not involve counting camels?"

Miles smiled. "Perhaps. This man, the Saracen who would take our God, gather the men and stay close to him, Thomas. Something is afoot. I do not trust the Hospitallers. I believe the prince may be about to enter into a dangerous folly."

The Templar enclave was surprisingly empty, when Miles arrived. All who were not tasked by Hugh had been enticed to view the rag-taggle and bizarre, as provided by Maleficius' troupe. Miles reined his horse and paused to watch as Edmund, one of a handful of remaining servants, struggled with a stack of heavy armour, his skinny arms trembling beneath the weight. The boy was a swift learner, there was no denying that. Diligent and earnest, he was at pains to avoid any doubt over his suitability for the job, but even so, he was a runt by any standard and Miles wondered whether he was strong enough to survive the long journey home.

Edmund's outward journey from England may have been blighted by his former master's cruelty but at least then he had been in the company of others, an entourage of many, where the boy's lack of size and strength were not greatly to his disadvantage. Miles suspected that the lad had used guile to avoid the tasks that were beyond his physical capabilities, and indeed that was to his credit. He'd suffered enough at the hands of Guy-de-Marchant without adding further to his ordeal. But the fact remained, when the time came for their eventual departure from The Holy Land the trip would be most arduous and there would be no one to lift and carry for him.

"Enough, Edmund, we shall all grow old from waiting. Leave the armour. I shall see to it."

"But, yer shoulder, my lord?"

Miles flexed his left arm and rotated his shoulder carefully. His altercation with Jesmina had certainly not helped matters. On the surface the wound was all but healed, a credit to Hugh's skill with suture and a hot blade but deep inside the nagging pain still bothered him.

The fact that his enemy Marchant was responsible and had still not been held to task, did not sit well. He'd given Guy an ultimatum, leave Acre or suffer the consequences. Miles could only assume, as his enemy had not been seen since, that he'd taken heed of the warning, packed up his band of mercenaries and slunk away. Even so, he knew with certainty that Guy's disappearance did not mean an end to the matter. The denouement was merely postponed, a period which enabled his own recovery, but also allowed Guy to re-group and plot anew.

He banished thoughts of Guy and smiled at the boy. "My shoulder? A scratch, Edmund, nothing more. Worry not, I can still swing a sword or indeed lift a battered breast plate if the need arises. But first, I seek Sir Hugh's council. Do you know where I might find him?"

Edmund screwed up his face as if he were considering a great many places where Hugh might be found. Miles bit back his impatience. The walls of Acre could fall, the Saracen hordes could drive them into the sea and all the while the child dithered and dawdled.

"He spoke of a meeting," Miles prompted, "do you know with whom he meets?"

"Maleficius..." The boy slapped a hand tight across his own mouth, as if the name had slipped out unbidden and he was at pains to conceal his fascination of the strange man and his collection of wondrous beasts.

"Edmund, I care not if you wish to ogle at the menagerie. As long as your duties are complete you may join the urchins and half-wits who drool at the caged beasts and performing idiots. I only wish to locate Hugh - as a matter of urgency."

The boy drew a breath, clearly unsure whether he was considered a half-wit too. He was determined to prove that he wasn't. "Nay my lord, it is not meself who meets with the magician, but Sir Hugh. He wished to speak about the men who breathe fire and the giants on their wooden legs."

Miles shook his head. He could not begin to understand the need for Hugh to involve himself in such mundane matters, unless he believed the fire-eaters intended to burn down the royal pavilion, which was possible but highly unlikely. "And is he there now?"

Edmund scratched at his head. "Nay, my lord. Now he meets another."

"Another?" Miles wondered whether Jesmina had deliberately misled him, and she and Hugh were already ensconced, discussing matters which had little to do with the needs of security and more to do with Jesmina's desires. He discounted that notion as quickly as it came to him.

"V...Ve...Vel...." Edmund continued, struggling to get his tongue around an unfamiliar name. He raised a grubby hand and counted down his fingers.

One - Maleficius.

Two - Vel..."

"Veloque?" Surely Hugh would not take counsel from Henri-de-Veloque. The Hospitaller was known for his robust condemnation of the Templars and the two men had been at odds publicly and privately since the Templar's arrival in Acre. "Does Sir Hugh visit The Knights Hall?"

Edmund shrugged his skinny shoulders. "He will return presently," he announced, aping Hugh's formality in a high-pitched childish tone. Miles smiled as the boy folded down his third finger.

"Three - Ye must await him here."

The boy's relief that he had recalled all three messages of import and was not required to pronounce the Hospitaller's name was evident as he blew out an exasperated breath through pursed lips. The spluttered sound drew the attention of the horses tethered nearby. They flicked their ears, extending their necks toward him in the hope that the encouraging sound would be followed by a morsel to eat. Edmund flexed his blistered fingers, displaying his empty palms as if to negate the beasts' enquiry.

Miles nodded distractedly. Whatever Hugh's business with Veloque, his benefactor would not linger at The Knights Hall. In the interim he could do little but wait as he had been instructed, but the delay was unfortunate. He dare not leave Jesmina unaccompanied for long. Who knew what mischief she might initiate?

Miles turned his attention back to the boy and considered the pile of armour that had grown mysteriously throughout the day. He suspected that his own men had taken advantage of the lad's willingness to please. They had all taken him under their wing, protective of the new addition to their order, but still not above pushing a jest to the extreme. The lad had risen to the challenge, but it was time to call a halt.

"Leave the armour," repeated Miles as he dismounted. "You've polished it within an inch of its life. Let's hope I dazzle my enemies before they come within striking distance, for you've taken half the thickness of metal away with the cloth. Take a brush to my horse instead, Edmund, while I wait for Hugh, and when you've finished with the feathers at his feet and the swing of his tail, find a box to stand on and see to his mane. Coquet is in a sorry state and the celebrations are about to begin."

"Coquet? Why do ye name him so?" The boy reached up to tangle his fingers in the horse's thick mane. "Surely Valiant or Blade would be more fitting."

Miles extended his hand and the great beast nuzzled him, snorting through velvet nostrils. He hushed the horse with a few whispered words, aware that Edmund watched curiously. That a knight who had vanquished so many could show such gentleness was a conundrum to most, but to Miles it made perfect sense. The horse had carried him fearlessly, had stood over him protectively when he had fallen in battle. They enjoyed a closeness and a respect that many would never understand.

"He is named for the river that flows through the domain of my birth. In winter the water swells orange with pride and roars through the valley carrying whole trees in its wake..."

"And boys?" Edmund's eyes were wide.

"And boys if they are foolish enough to dip their feet in its waters."

"And in summer?"

"In summer, you may kick off your shoes and paddle among the rocks, or swim in the deep pools. And when Autumn colours cloak the woods, great fish swim in the current."

"I wish to see this great river, my lord."

"And so you shall, Edmund. Soon we shall leave this place and head for home. The great trading ships anchor in the harbour awaiting the tide. We shall be on the very next one I promise you that, but first we must accommodate the prince's birthday wish. He has a fancy for another spectacle and who are we to disappoint him."

Edmund drew the back of a grubby horse-scented hand across his face and lowered his voice to a whisper.

"Have ye seen the beast, my lord?"

Miles knew there were many beasts in Acre and most wore armour, but the lad was clearly awe-struck by another.

"Which beast would that be, Edmund?"

Edmund squatted by one of the horse's great feet and began to brush the tangles from his feathered fetlock. As the massive horse closed its eyes and slumbered in the soft glow of the setting sun, Edmund turned his attention back to Miles.

"The el-ee-phant. A giant beast. Taller than a camel and wider than an ox. It has a nose as long as a man's arm, longer indeed, and feet the size of ..." he splayed his hands wide to demonstrate, "...a Mamluk's shield."

Miles had indeed seen the elephant and all the other exotic animals intended as the centre piece of Edward's celebration. Corralled outside the city, they had been paraded into Acre that morning to the accompaniment of the troubadours. Some of the creatures were so strange he wondered whether there was mischief afoot, yet more trickery to fool the onlookers. Perhaps beneath the stripes and speckles and horns and spines, were mere donkeys or dogs appended for the benefit of the gullible. Or perhaps, as some would believe, they were the creations of sorcery, heretic's weapons wielded by the devil himself.

The man Maleficius had attracted a reputation which was at odds with his attendance at a Christian prince's celebration. The church would ring its hands, debate the choice and either turn a blind eye, or condemn, whichever was most advantageous, and Miles was not about to wager the outcome. There were enough relics in Acre to protect the prince should the need arise.

Thomas maintained that along with the elephant he had seen a milk-white unicorn, its mane, pale gold in the moonlight. Miles wasn't convinced at that and now having been witness to the beauty of Jesmina's cob-webbed stallion he wagered the beasts were one in the same. In any event Thomas liked to spin a tale and since the boy had joined their company, he had taken great relish in entertaining and scaring the lad.

"What do ye think a great beast like that eats?" asked Edmund with a worried frown.

"Boys, Edmund. Boys who chatter when they should be working," replied Miles impatiently. "Now, it seems that if I am to engage with Sir Hugh before the festivities begin, I must seek him at The Knights Hall. Tend to Coquet. See that he is well watered. I fear I may have need of a swift horse before the night is out.

Three

It was evident to Miles as he made his way on foot through gloomy thoroughfares that something was amiss. Night would soon be upon them and the rush of incomers had subsided, but in place of the frantic anticipation that had filled the streets there was a strange sense of foreboding. Unsure whether it was simply his meeting with Jesmina that unsettled him, or the risk associated with the prince's ill-advised festivities, he hurried on regardless. He ignored the beggars' outstretched arms, the constant demands of the feral urchins, and his own simmering disquiet.

Keeping out of sight, he skirted the main arena. The place was already filled to capacity, though the entertainment was not scheduled to begin until dusk. The traders slipped through the crowd hawking their wares aggressively and the spectators, cross-legged on the sand, were easy prey. Bone tired and hungry, they bartered what little they had in exchange for spiced lamb and sweetmeats and settled themselves to await the festivities. From the shadows beneath the stands, the muffled roars and bellows of restrained beasts filtered through, drawing fearful gasps from those positioned close enough to hear. Miles inhaled, the air was heavy with incense and spiced with intrigue.

The darkening sky reminded Miles that time was pressing if he were to complete his task as requested. The prince's arrival was imminent, as was Hugh's, and Miles must deliver his message first. If Jesmina were to grow impatient and make her presence known, she would endanger Hugh whether she intended it or not.

Known to the Hospitallers, Miles had fought alongside them and on occasion against them. He hoped the sentry on the gate did not recall their last encounter and approached The Knights Hall with a ready-made excuse on his lips as to why he required admittance. He faltered when activity drew his eye to the shadows to the left of the main gate. Hugh stood in conversation with another whose back was turned. By the cross of St John emblazoned on his black cloak, Miles could only assume Hugh's companion was none other than Henri-de-Veloque.

The senior Hospitaller leaned in close as if he strained to hear Hugh's hushed tone. Miles edged closer too, also keen to listen in, but before he could improve his position, the men straightened and Hugh extended a hand which was firmly clasped by Veloque. The men embraced formally, a deal no doubt, though Miles could only wonder at the detail. As Veloque retreated into the fortress and the massive gate slammed shut, Miles stepped out of the shadows.

"Hugh, you are a difficult man to locate. I have scoured Acre and where do I find you, but rubbing shoulders with a man who would sell us all to the devil."

Hugh's narrowed eyes betrayed his irritation at Miles' sudden appearance. It was obvious that he had not wished a witness to his alliance with Veloque, which begged the question – why? Hugh was many things, to many people and most, including Miles, were unclear as to his true purpose, nevertheless even he was surprised at this turn of events.

Hugh pushed past, his eye to the dipping sun and the late hour. "If you have time to scour Acre then I obviously do not employ you fully," he muttered. "I must remedy that."

Miles raised a long-suffering brow. He was well used to the sharp edge of Hugh's tongue. "I trawl the streets on your behalf, sir. In fact I carry a message from a friend."

"Indeed." Hugh took him roughly by the arm and bundled him out of sight of the Hospitaller guards. "We must not linger here. Come, let us make haste. I wager there is much to do before this ridiculous spectacle is at an end. Edward must wonder at my absence."

"Not so. The torches are lit. The troubadours fiddle with pipes and string, and the heretic Maleficius grows impatient," replied Miles. "He paces like a demi-god while his animals bellow and writhe at their chains. The great showman is poised to astound the crowds but Edward is delayed and the crowd grow restless."

"Watch your tongue, Miles," snapped Hugh. "There are no heretics in Acre – do you hear?"

Miles frowned. Hugh's agitation was misplaced and out of character. Ordinarily the man was in complete control. He quickened his pace as they took a short cut through the darkened alley at the rear of the covered market. Miles raised a hand, in an effort to steer his mentor toward the spice-traders stall and Jesmina, but Hugh was determined to reach the royal apartments before the curfew sounded and marched on regardless.

"Edward is delayed, you say?"

"He toys with his new gift, no doubt."

"Gift?" barked Hugh.

"Baybars' man, who wishes to carry The Cross. Was he not the subject of your discourse with Veloque? Surely the man did not miss the opportunity to explain how his goodly knights found a convert for the prince while we poor Templars were otherwise engaged counting goats." Miles could not disguise his chagrin.

"You jest surely?" Hugh pinned him with a sharp look.

"I do not, more's the pity. Edward seeks to parade the man along with the elephant and dancing dogs. Personally

I do not see the sense of it, but the prince will have his way no doubt."

Hugh frowned. "Why was I not informed? An enemy is allowed within reach of the prince and no one thinks to relay this information to me. No one deems the action to be risky?"

"No one could find you, Hugh. It seems your man Veloque has kept you busy while the Hospitallers steal your glory."

"Miles, you miss the thrill of the battlefield, are clearly not suited to the mundane minutiae of a soldier's life, or the politic that puts food on your platter, but please don't allow your boredom to cloud your vision. You amuse yourself by inventing allegiances and subterfuge where there are none. Meanwhile the obvious and important detail, which you appear to have overlooked, is not the fact that I discuss business with Veloque, or even that the Hospitallers have stolen a pace on us, but that Baybars' men would rather pull out their own eyes and feed them to the vultures than turn their back on their prophet. This is clearly a plot that reeks of Saracen cunning." He glanced back over his shoulder as if he feared assassins stalked the shadows. "It remains to be seen whether Veloque or his knights are a party to this or merely tools of another. Make haste, Miles. I fear nothing good will come of this."

In the arena the gathered crowds grew restless, bored with the banal and hungry for spectacle. Hundreds of feet stamped in unison and what began as a good natured noisy protest, soon developed into a situation that required deft handling. Hugh barked orders right and left and the crowd of mounted knights awaiting their turn to parade, parted to allow Hugh's unhindered progress to the prince's chambers. At the entrance he turned and gripped Miles' jerkin tightly, pulling him close.

"Seek out Maleficius, ensure that he begins his ridiculous show without delay or this crowd will become a mob. Make the necessary excuses for Edward's lateness..."

"What shall I say?"

"Anything, Miles. Use your imagination. Just ensure the jesters jest, the jugglers juggle, and the giant beasts perform their ghoulish theatre and distract the mass of gawking fools, before the good folk of Acre decide to create their own entertainment at our expense."

"And what of Jesmina?" Miles called after Hugh as the man released his grip and strode away.

"Jesmina?" The older knight's stride faltered.

"The message...she seeks a meeting."

"Here in Acre?" Hugh frowned, the prince and his convert momentarily forgotten. "You're mistaken. Jesmina would not come here. It's not prudent or safe."

"I'm not mistaken. She waits for you by the church of St John. I tried to explain to her that you were otherwise engaged and that she was not safe. *She* would not listen. I tried to explain to you about her, about the message. *You* would not listen. I explain to one and all and no one listens and meanwhile mischief tracks our footsteps like the devil's jester."

"Why does she seek me?"

"She refused to say." Miles recalled his failed attempts to discover her purpose. "She was most insistent that she speak only to you."

"And you accepted such folly?"

"Not willingly. Jesmina is not an easy subject. She distracts..."

Hugh shook his head wryly. "Jesmina plays a game with all who cross her path. The woman has designs on me that unfortunately do not match my own."

Miles shrugged his agreement. "Perhaps, yet she was *most* insistent. She plans to seek you here in the royal pavilion if you fail to meet her at the church. I believe she will do that, Hugh, and in light of the current situation," he cast an arm to encompass the growing impatience of the crowd, "that might not be wise."

Hugh stepped away, obviously torn by the need to quash any Hospitaller mischief-making and nullify any possible threat to the prince, but interested nonetheless in Jesmina's arrival. He studied Miles through narrowed eyes. "Did she say nothing, no clue as to her purpose?"

"Only that her father was inordinately busy today. Her words, not mine."

"Her father?" Hugh cursed aloud. "I doubt very much that Saladin intends to entertain the prince by charming snakes from a basket. If he is busy then he is trading poison and Jesmina thinks we should be made aware."

"Perhaps she alludes to the information you await regarding St George-de-Lebeyre?"

"Nay, I think not. Saladin is as slippery, as his daughter is desirable. He plies his trade to the highest bidder, and there is no one higher than Baybars, but I have no time now to unravel his deceit. Where are the men?"

"Thomas gathers them as we speak. They are enroute to protect the prince."

"Good. So you sense it too?"

Miles nodded. "I sense a collision of a great many things this evening, whether by happenstance or design I have no idea, but my skin crawls with apprehension."

Hugh reached out and patted Miles' shoulder roughly. "You have a keen instinct, Miles, as do I. In this instance let's hope we are both wrong. Use Maleficius, the man is a master at persuasion, the crowd must be calmed and he is the one to do it. And then, when the magician has the beasts and the believers in thrall, send the boy to Jesmina and have him bring her to me."

"Here?"

"Yes. All eyes will be on the spectacle. Wait beneath the pavilion I will meet you there. But I urge you to handle her with care, Miles. The woman has much to lose and courts more danger than you can possibly imagine."

The man, Maleficius, was a sight to be marvelled at – from a prudent distance. His hair, jet black, descended to his waist. His nose hooked, his eyes protruding and red-rimmed, he had the qualities of a giant hooded crow and the temperament to match. He pulled his blood red cloak tight around his skeletal frame and scowled at Miles.

"I am no pox-ridden serf who exists simply to carry out your bidding," he snapped his response to Miles' request, his head bobbing sharply as if he meant to peck. Miles took a cautious step back, unsure quite how to tackle such an oddity. Hugh had spoken of him with some measure of respect, the boy Edmund was in thrall of him, but Miles was less convinced. His sense of unease increased and he crossed himself discreetly.

"It is not my bidding, but that of Sir Hugh-de-Reynard."

Maleficius' mouth curled into a lop-sided grimace, an unsuccessful attempt at a sly smile distorted by a vicious scar that dissected the black-painted upper lip in two. Miles could not drag his eyes away. The man's teeth could be seen quite clearly through the gap. They were filed to jagged points.

"Ah, the Fox." Maleficius turned swiftly and a hand shot out from beneath his velveteen garments to cuff the ear of a wizened dwarf who lagged behind the troupe. The shrunken man was bizarrely dressed in animal skins. His gnarled face, thick with grease and dye, resembled a nightmarish mating of fur and fowl. Antlers sprang from his leather hood, peacock feathers extended from his sleeves. He cursed in an unfamiliar language before pasting on a hideous grin and scurrying after his comrades.

"The prince is delayed with matters of state. Hugh simply asks that you use your undoubted skill to forestall the impatient rabble in his absence. Look upon it as a prequel to the main event. I'm sure you have minstrels and idiots aplenty."

"Skill?" Maleficius cocked his head and stepped close. Miles could feel his rancid breath, hot against his cheek. His hand strayed to the dagger at his waist, but he resisted the overwhelming urge to use it.

"Yes, I understand you are without equal when it comes to spectacle. Your beasts are trained to shock, your idiots to entertain...."

"And sorcery, what do you hear of that?"

The man had the strangest eyes. Perhaps it was merely the torchlight that gave them such a golden hue, nevertheless Miles averted his own. He had no wish to be hexed. "You would do well to guard your tongue, magician. You may currently be in the prince's favour, you might well have earned the dubious respect of Sir Hugh, though it puzzles me to understand why, but if you speak of magic and dark arts in a city held by men sworn to The Cross, then you risk more than your life."

Maleficius laughed; a wet gurgle that boiled up from a cauldron deep inside. He turned his head and spat his venom onto the sand. "Templar, look to your own before you cast doubt on others. Your brothers reek of the unholy, cross or no cross. I do not fear for my life, Miles of Wildewood. Nor do I intend to jeopardise my *family*. Can you say the same?"

The man picked at scabs that were not yet healed, yet despite the risk, Miles was drawn by the lure of the unspoken. "You know my name."

"Your name and considerably more, *honourable* knight." He tapped his hooked beak conspiratorially.

"How? We have never met. Do you speak of me with friend or foe?" Miles' mind filled suddenly with images best forgotten and he shook his head to be rid of them. This man, this macabre creation could not possibly know his darkest secrets – unless the Templar oath was broken or his nemesis remained in Acre after all. Perhaps instead of returning to Lincoln with his tail between his legs, Guy lurked in dark corners stirring the pot of malcontent.

"You have enemies who would seek to discredit you?" asked Maleficius.

"Don't we all?"

"Ah, yes. The unenlightened, perhaps we are not so different after all. But to your credit, young knight, you are not without your supporters, those who follow blindly regardless of your inglorious past."

"You talk in riddles."

"Not so. A little bird tweets in my ear, his feathers puffed with pride...the brave knight, the wounded knight, the knight who dreams of another place, of deeds and dire consequences."

"Edmund?" Miles scowled. He must teach the boy the value of silence.

"The boy is your conscience, treasure him. One day he will save you, as you have saved him."

The man was a showman, an entertainer, a spinner of tall tales and make-believe, even so Miles was unnerved. "You know nothing of me," he hissed as he edged back, confused, unsure whether the man had real purpose or was merely cursed with a love of dark mischief and an unfortunate manner.

"Time will tell. When next we meet we shall see whether my words have substance or not. But now at your demand, I must attend to the crowd who slaver like rabid dogs." He turned on his heel, his cloak billowing about him as he strode out into the torch-lit arena, his staff held high as if he sought a lightning bolt to quell the crowds. And as if by some mystical force the crowd did grow silent and anticipation hung heavy in the air.

Miles watched, bemused, as the man was followed by a procession of brightly coloured wagons of various sizes. The larger hauled by oxen, the smaller by pairs of miniature ponies, their manes and tails dyed red to match the magician's cloak. Cackling jesters teased their flanks with the tip of a whip. The little ponies whinnied angrily and stamped their tiny hooves, while inside the caged wagons, hidden behind painted shutters, the wild beasts awaited Maleficius' grand reveal.

Miles retreated to the shadows and scanned the arena from his concealed position. The crowd's attention was solely on Maleficius. Their anticipation tightly wound by the promise of the weird and wondrous and their fear of the consequences. No one paid any heed to an altercation brewing at the far corner of the arena but Miles attention was drawn straight to it. He recognised the white tabard and red cross of his own men as they sought passage past the black cloaked Hospitallers. *Damn them.* If his men could not access the royal apartments, then Hugh was quite alone in ensuring the prince's safety. Miles stepped back with a muttered curse as the elephant lumbered past with a swaying gait. On its back, a child with skin as black as ebony flashed a white toothed grin. Between the legs of the giant beast Miles caught sight of the recipient of the greeting, lurking in the shadows. He waited to allow the beast to pass safely then shot out a hand and caught the eavesdropper by the scruff of his neck.

"Edmund, just the boy I seek. I have urgent business for you."

The child grinned sheepishly. "I only wished to see the animals. There are tigers and lions and monkeys dressed as men. Ye said I could watch..."

"Indeed you may, but first I have need of your swift feet." Miles shot a suspicious glance at the brightly garbed entertainers who awaited their turn in the ring. They hovered close, their interest unwanted. He stooped low and whispered hoarsely into the boy's ear. "Run to the spice-traders. Do not stop. There you will find the lady Jesmina. Bring her here by way of the darkest alleys. Do not reveal your purpose to anyone. Do you hear? No one."

"Jesmi -?"

Miles slapped a hand firmly over the boy's mouth and squeezed tightly. "Listen, little man. Believe me when I say that this is of the utmost importance. Sir Hugh demands this of you. The prince may be in danger. We may all be in danger. Go now and prove your worth. And remember, Edmund, speak to no one of your task."

Once released, the boy was off like a hare, darting through the timber framework of the pavilion, ducking under the bellies of horses and between the gangly wooden legs of the stilt-walkers. Miles watched until he was out of sight. When convinced the boy had not been waylaid, he pushed his way through the tumbling acrobats and scanned the crowd again. The altercation between the rival knights had escalated, drawing curious glances. As the onlookers were pushed back by the threat of entanglement, the barriers heaved to breaking point threatening to spill the discontent into the arena. Miles cursed. Ordinarily if a fight were imminent he would have been first to raise a fist and Thomas could be relied upon as peacemaker, but where the knights of St John were concerned he doubted the matter would be settled promptly.

Maleficius drew the crowd's attention back to the centre of the arena with the unveiling of the first of the caged wagons. Hoots of raucous laughter greeted the sight of ten or more monkeys dressed as lords and ladies of the royal court. Miles doubted the creatures shared their mirth as they were bound to each other with a tether tight about each furred wrist. Released from their cage, they paraded hand-in-hand in a sorry line. The crowd applauded their comical antics, but Miles suspected the frozen grimace on each monkey's face had little to do with enjoyment and more with fear. He used the distraction of their theatre and the cover of the wagons and ran across the centre of the arena. The Templars were required urgently at the prince's side and the fight must be stopped.

Four

Miles forced his way between men who had riled themselves into such a state they were ready to draw swords on each other. "For pity's sake, desist!" He grabbed hold of the nearest black cloaked Hospitaller by the shoulder and swung him around, receiving a gloved fist to his jaw for his trouble. As he struggled back to his feet two of his own men rallied to his defence. "Where is Thomas?" he called as he dodged another blow. The man was not present and Miles could only assume that he had not delivered the call to arms.

"With the prince," grunted a bloodied Templar, "we delay only to teach these harbinger's a lesson. The sons of whores believe they have the right to bar our way."

"You do not have time to sharpen your blades on Hospitaller skulls, leave this nonsense for another day."

The Templar laughed, "What? You have no stomach for a fight, Miles? You must sicken, surely."

"Later, William, first we must attend to the prince." He ducked as another blow narrowly missed him, but this time he was ready and caught his assailant by the wrist twisting it fiercely until the knight was forced to his knees. "You wish to take this further?" he hissed, "and I will gladly oblige, later, in the arena, with a weapon of your choice." The man snarled as Miles yanked his face-guard free.

Miles started back with alarm, confusion slowing his initial response. The man was not a Hospitaller. His swarthy complexion betrayed his true identity as one of Baybars' followers.

"We are betrayed!" Miles' urgent yell stopped his knights, in mid blow. For a moment the men's shock at the deceit held them frozen. The imposters, freed from subterfuge, threw off their helmets, shed their cloaks and from beneath their dusty robes, drew the short curved swords favoured by the Saracens. As reality bullied disbelief away, the Templars reciprocated and what had begun as an age old rivalry between fellows, transformed into a bloody fight. Miles struggled to keep hold of the man within his grasp. He squirmed and thrashed like a wild animal. Too close to draw anything other than a knife they wrestled, each one determined to thwart the other.

"What is planned?" hissed Miles as he gained the upper hand, and forced the man to the ground beneath him. He pressed the tip of his blade ever closer to the man's throat, held at bay only by the strength of the Saracen's grip tight at his wrist. The man spat in his face, disarming Miles momentarily as he blinked the spittle away. In that moment the man seized his opportunity, dealt a crippling blow to Miles' injured shoulder and wriggled free. Scrabbling desperately after him, Miles gained his feet but lost the man. Within an instant he was gone, his comrades fleeing with him, lost quickly within the crowds of similarly robed spectators like ghostly apparitions. In the air the lingering insult of Saracen curses mingled with the cheers from the arena. On the ground the scattered cloaks of fallen men lay like empty shadows. Somewhere amidst Acre's darkening shroud the mortal remains of the slain Hospitallers would no doubt be discovered. Miles had no great love for the rival knights but in this regard his stomach churned with the need for revenge on their behalf.

He dragged in a breath and stooped to retrieve his knife. Above them, high in the pavilion, oblivious to the narrowly avoided threat, the horns sounded to announce the prince's arrival. The Templars stood down, confusion swiftly replaced by relief when realisation of a disaster averted by luck rather than good planning dawned. There would be time enough to avenge the Hospitaller deaths after the festivities. They gathered their weapons, checked their wounds and in the absence of Thomas, turned to Miles for direction.

Miles swung his gaze slowly from the bloodied men to the royal dais. The prince was not yet seated. In his place attendants scurried like so many headless fowl. There was something amiss, though Miles could not determine the cause. He scanned right and left. The prince's chosen guests were seated, the Saracen threat averted ... and yet. Suddenly, as if a rabid beast approached, the crowds parted and Thomas hurtled toward him, descending the wooden pavilion steps two at a time, stumbling, righting himself and all the while gesticulating wildly. Fearful spectators scrambled frantically to avoid him. A tangible wave of alarm swept the crowd and by the time Thomas reached him, the message was clear, no matter the language.

"Edward...," Thomas gulped a breath. He grabbed at Miles' jerkin and held fast. His whole body trembled with shock and exertion. Miles reached out and supported him as his legs threatened to give way.

"Steady, man. What in God's name has happened?"

"Edward - a mortal wound - an assassin!"

"Where, how..." Miles swung around wildly. The Templars gathered close, weapons drawn, but Thomas waved them away impatiently.

"The convert – a concealed knife - Hugh is with the prince now. Eleanor is distraught. They fear the worse."

"And the man, the assassin, is he apprehended?" Miles shook Thomas vigourously. A scream from the crowd was all the reply he needed. The imposter, pursued by armed guards fled through the crowd scattering onlookers in his wake. The guards were impeded by the sheer mass of people. The assassin took advantage, scrambled over the barrier and raced for the exit.

Miles pushed Thomas aside and set off in pursuit. Scrambling past panicked spectators, he vaulted the wooden barrier that held back the crowds, landing with a grunt on the other side. Before him, the disorderly mass of Maleficius' troupe obscured his view and threatened to slow his progress. He cared not if the stilt-walkers toppled one upon the other or the shrunken ponies stampeded as he ploughed through them, but the chaos and noise disoriented him. He spun around and shot an urgent look at Thomas, positioned atop the barrier. The knight gestured wildly toward the far side of the arena. The lone assassin covered the ground in loping strides. His billowing white robes marked red with the prince's blood.

Miles drew his knife and quickened his pace. He was closing the gap. He must not let the assassin escape. Once free from the confines of the arena he would, like his Saracen fellows, simply disappear. The elephant lumbered into his path trumpeting loudly, and Miles ducked beneath its swaying belly, his speed barely checked, his confidence growing. He would have the man and have a blade at his throat before he'd managed another dozen paces. But suddenly he was falling, his feet entangled amid the troupe of tethered monkeys. They scrabbled at him wildly. Shrieking in distress as they also tumbled, hands held tightly, caps and skirts askew. Miles grabbed the nearest by its skinny arm and sliced his blade through the tether at its wrist. "Be gone, devils," he cursed and the animals, as if possessed with human instinct, loosed each other one by one and ran free.

The assassin faltered, as fire-breathers directed the flames to thwart his escape. He changed direction only to run directly into the side of one of the larger cages, driven with purpose into his path. Maleficius stood poised on its roof his staff held high. He yelled his orders and his stunted acolytes slid the iron bolts free and pulled back the shutters. Inside the cage, a lion opened its massive jaws and roared. The Saracen lurched back from the bars and Miles scrambled to his feet, shook the last clinging monkey from his arm, and the crowd went wild.

"Miles!"

The urgent yell drew Miles attention, as all around him the entertainers and animals scattered. Thomas waved a frantic warning from the far barrier as Jesmina and Edmund looked on in horror from the entrance. Both were mounted on the prancing stallion, the boy clinging desperately to Jesmina's waist. The lion threw itself against the confines of the cage and the bars creaked ominously. Maleficius grinned, hideous and malformed, and the assassin turned on his heels and ran for his life.

Miles hesitated, now the fleeing Saracen was not his only concern. The lion, goaded further by the constant beating of Maleficius' staff on the roof of the cage, had been sent quite wild. It threw itself repeatedly against the weakened bars, lashed out its giant paws and rent the air with lethal claws. The crowd, whipped into frenzy by the promise of a spectacle like no other, began to chant furiously. Miles began to run, quite sure that either his lungs would burst with the effort of the chase or he would go mad with the manic din. Was this all a theatre orchestrated by the magician? Or was he doomed to die in the jaws of the very same beast that graced the banners of England?

"Miles!"

He sensed rather than heard Thomas' urgent demand and he shot another desperate glance over his shoulder. Thomas pointed a gloved hand. At the entrance Edmund slipped from the stallion's back and Jesmina raised her whip. He saw the flash of golden mane as the milk-white stallion, spurred on by Jesmina, leapt the barrier and rushed toward him. She either meant to mow him down or provide assistance. He decided upon the latter and reached out as the terrified beast thundered past. He caught

111

Jesmina's outstretched arm and hauled himself up behind her. The pain which ripped through his shoulder was naught compared to what he faced if the lion broke its confines.

Leaning close against Jesmina's body, Miles took the reins from her and urged the animal on. Cheered by the crowd, he put thoughts of all consequences to one side and bore down on the fleeing assassin. As the man made a final scramble for the exit, Miles launched himself from the stallion's back.

He heard the man's neck break when he fell upon him. Though gratified to have caught his prey, it brought him no joy to have delivered such a swift end.

Propelled directly from the arena to the royal apartments, Miles was neither willing nor prepared for a royal summons. The whole event was a jumble in his head and once again he suspected that he was not in possession of all the necessary details.

"Are you ready?" Hugh stood to one side and ran a disparaging glance over Miles' dishevelled state.

"Not entirely." An image of the snarling Maleficius crept into his head and he shot Hugh a puzzled look. What was the connection between the two?

"Later," said Hugh with a swift shake of the head, as if he read Miles thoughts and wished them silent.

"The prince will see you now." Edward's attendant interrupted. He dipped his head and backed away, one outstretched arm held the door to the royal chamber ajar.

Miles paused. He felt uncomfortable amongst the finery and defensive of the guarded looks his presence seemed to generate. Hugh patted his arm reassuringly, and with each throb from his still healing wound Miles was minded of his benefactor's skill. Without Hugh, he would surely have perished at Qaqun. With Hugh at his side, the prince might yet be saved, though talk amongst the courtiers and serving wenches was that the assassin's knife had dealt a fatal blow and would take Edward to the grave before the night was out.

"Take heed, Miles," muttered Hugh. "Speak only when necessary. Answer with caution. The prince is plagued with delirium and fed by those who would do us ill. The physicians argue, Eleanor weeps and the royal house is in turmoil."

"What can I do? Why am I here?"

"The prince asks for you, that alone suggests a glimmer of hope in an otherwise dismal situation."

The chamber was poorly lit. To Miles, the flickering light merely extenuated the horror of the situation. Edward was propped up on his pillows. Fever added a fiery hue to an otherwise grey pallor. Attendants dithered and physicians looked on sagely. Miles filtered a shallow breath through clenched teeth. There was an unfortunate odour about the place, a cocktail of incense and decay that caught the back of his throat and made his stomach roll unpleasantly. He longed to step back into the shadows where he could hide his revulsion, but instead he stood his ground and addressed the future king.

"Sire." He bowed and waited, uncertain whether Edward was conscious or capable of discourse. The prince's eyes rolled open and despite his obvious state of malaise the eyes were sharp and calculating.

"These men about me, these surgeons in their wisdom seek to bleed the very life from me. What say you, Miles of Wildewood?"

Miles shrugged. The physicians stood ready with blade and bowl. He could neither recommend nor discredit their remedy, but recognised Hugh's disapproval by his rigid stance and tightly clenched fists. "You asked to see me, sire."

"Indeed. I fear I am not long for this world. I seek to reward those who have served me. And, Miles, you have served me well. The assassin, I understand he is dead thanks to you."

"And my fellow Templars, sire. I did not act alone."

Edward shifted his gaze momentarily to Hugh and smiled. "Ah yes, my trusted Templars. You have all served me well, both here in my hour of need and before when others would have balked. Yet there is much more to do...and not the time to do it."

"I am your servant, sire, always," said Miles, for want of something better to say. If Edward died, England would mourn but he would be free from a debt that he feared he'd never be able to repay, not in this life or the next. He shuffled uncomfortably and was edged aside by the physicians, their disapproval of his lowly status evident as they tutted and grumbled.

"Sire, you are not strong," murmured the nearest. His course apron was stained with royal blood, his finger nails black with filth. "We must continue if we are to expel the evil that rages within."

Edward raised one hand impatiently. "Enough, I am an empty vessel. Leave me in peace for pity's sake."

"But, sire..."

"Enough!" He thrust out a surprisingly strong hand and caught the physician's bowl. Blood, black and semi-congealed, spattered far and wide catching the physicians, the simpering attendants and the leather boots of the two knights. The learned men fled the room in horror, the servants scattered in shock, but Miles and Hugh, well used to the blood of men, stood their ground and Eleanor dried her eyes and smiled weakly at them.

"I must reward you, Miles, if I am to ensure entry to the heavens above. What can I bestow upon a knight who kills a royal assassin? Great wealth, fine horses, the hand of a beautiful maiden?"

"Your reward is not necessary, sire."

Edward heaved himself up a little and flicked a calculating glance between Miles and Hugh. "You guard your young knight well, Sir Hugh. I wager you coach his speech as well as his actions? Do you fear for him or me?"

"Neither, sire," murmured Hugh, his voice deliberately pitched low to fox those who pressed an ear to the door. "I worry though that you are not best served by your surgeons."

"And who are you to question men trained in the medicinal arts?"

"I have some skill in the area, sire. The lad is proof of that. Did I not repair him to fight again after Qaqun?"

The prince nodded and Eleanor reached out and clasped her husband's hand. Hope flickered where there had been none.

"And more recently - the tournament. The lad's shoulder was almost cleaved in two and yet here he is, fit and able to thwart the royal assassin."

"You are a soldier of repute, a tactician without equal, a trusted advisor, but a surgeon you are not, despite evidence to the contrary."

"And is that not to your advantage, sire? Did your great uncle, Richard, not perish at the hands of a surgeon?"

Eleanor began to sob quietly. Miles edged toward the door. Hugh risked them all with claims that he was better equipped to treat the prince than the royal surgeons, even if the claim were true. There was no question the man was skilled, but if he tried and failed there would be no forgiving consolatory embrace, more likely a noose around his neck and the necks of all those who rode with him. If he succeeded, of course he would win the approval of the future monarch, a substantial prize in uncertain times, but equally he would garner the suspicion of the church and all those who believed the rumours of the Templar's association with the dark arts. It seemed that they were cursed no matter which way the die was cast. He wanted to reach out, to take Hugh's arm and pull him away. He wanted to beseech that he leave well alone, leave Edward to God and his physicians and in doing so free them all from the Templar oath that bound them to the prince with ever-tightening twine.

115

"Hugh," he cautioned hoarsely.

"I merely seek to check the state of the wound, sire," continued Hugh. "To assess the damage done and perhaps suggest a more successful remedy."

"I did not request your presence simply to discount the skill of the physicians who tend me," wheezed Edward.

"Let him try," pleaded Eleanor. "Please husband. Let him try. He speaks of success while your physicians whisper of failure."

Edward turned wearily to Miles. "Your reward, you'd best name it now. My physicians seek to bleed me dry, your benefactor seeks to alter the course of history and I am sorely tempted to allow him, if only to silence a weeping wife."

Miles stepped forward. His reluctance to be further indebted to the prince balanced by his very real desire to be out of the room and away from the cloying stench. "If it pleases you, sire, if you insist, I would take but one thing."

"And what would that be?"

"Wildewood, The domain and house of my birth."

"Is it not yours by title?"

"The situation is complicated, sire."

"Complicated?" Edward winced and Eleanor mopped at his perspiring brow. "I have neither patience nor time for *complicated*. Who complicates the matter?"

"Gerard-de-Frouville, sire."

"Ah, Frouville, my father's baron holds the border well. He keeps our Scottish cousins at bay. Like you, he also seeks to serve his future king. I see no complication there. Wildewood, for what it's worth, is yours. I will see that it is written. Does that suit you, Miles?"

Did it suit him? Indeed it did, but all the same Miles couldn't ignore the voice in his head that urged caution. Was this favour just another bind to tie him to a life he was trying to escape? At some future date would he and his fellow knights be paraded like the tethered monkeys for the benefit of a baying crowd. Aware that all eyes were upon him he simply nodded his agreement and backed away. Hugh stopped him with a firm grip on his arm. He pulled him close and leaned in to whisper hoarsely in his ear.

"Where is Jesmina?"

Miles shrugged. He had not seen her since leaping from her horse. "She was in the arena. She came to my assistance on her stallion." He smiled at the memory. "Now there is an animal to covet."

"The Sultan's stallion?"

"I believe so."

"Alas discretion is not a concept that Jesmina is familiar with. The horse will mark her out to those who seek and those who hunt."

"There is a difference?"

"Of course. Find her. She holds the key to this." Hugh gestured to the recumbent prince.

"You believe she is involved?" Miles frowned.

"Do you not smell it? The whole chamber reeks of decay – and poison."

"You suspect her?"

"I suspect she may be able to help. Where there is poison there is antidote and if anyone in this land would know of it I wager Jesmina to be the one. Go now. Find her, and find her quickly. I fear the future king does not have long."

Five

Hugh was correct. In assisting Miles so publicly, Jesmina had placed herself at great risk. Those within the crowd who supported Baybars would report her traitorous action back to the Sultan, while those who coveted Hugh's unique position within the royal court would question this dubious liaison. Jesmina must be swiftly located for the sake of all concerned. The prince's survival, as well as her own, depended upon it.

Miles, glad to be free of the stench of decay, took a long breath and scanned the dawn streets. He quickly located Thomas who bore the look of a man who'd spent the night hunched in a doorway with naught but a cloak for comfort.

"Did you lose a woman or a wager, Thomas?"

The weary knight opened his eyes and shook himself awake. "Neither. I simply stand watch in case the tide turns against my fellow Templars. There is an undercurrent of mistrust that grows unabated, within and without these walls. I feel it in my bones. How does the prince fare?"

Miles shrugged. He felt it too, the feeling that a mighty storm was headed their way. Morning had brought with it a post-coital regret to Acre. There were no jugglers or jesters and the beasts were silent in their stalls. The pilgrims no longer filled the streets with anticipation, but moved quietly about their business as if an ominous cloud hung over all. Not for the first time, Miles wished that he were gone from the place. He took another deep breath, imagined he could scent the sea and prayed for a benevolent tide.

Taking Thomas by the arm, Miles herded him away from the eavesdroppers who lurked outside the royal apartments. He was not convinced that their business was innocent. "The prince lives - for now," he murmured as he leaned in closer "Thomas, tell me, do you know the whereabouts of Jesmina? I must thank her in person for yesterday."

Thomas brushed his hand away. He sent him a look, a reminder that despite repeated warnings, he still trod a dangerous path and had much to learn. "Jesmina? So it *was* she, back there in the market place. I thought as much. She was overly keen to assist you in the arena." He shook his head in disbelief. "But surely even you are not foolish enough to dabble with the wench who has stolen Hugh's eye."

Miles scowled. He had some work to do to improve his reputation. What did Thomas suppose he had *dabbled* with, in the time it had taken to pursue a suspect on horseback? He suspected he would have some explaining to do – but not to his fellow Templar. "No, Thomas, not foolish, though some would agree any association with that woman brings with it a certain risk."

"So you admit to an association?"

"Entirely innocent."

"There is talk."

"What have you heard?"

"Much. Nothing. Nonsense and yet..."

"Tell me."

"The wench is betwixt and between. She slips cunningly from one camp to another and one bed to another. She did herself no favours by assisting you yesterday. The Sultan's men seek her *and* the horse. Hugh will no doubt express his displeasure if it transpires you have also been indiscreet with the harlot."

"Thomas, for pity's sake, enough! This is not what you imagine. I have been indiscreet with no one. We must locate Jesmina. We need her most urgently. The prince's condition is grave, Hugh believes she may be the only one who can help and yet it appears she is hunted by both sides in this debacle. We must find her first."

"I fear that is not the least of our troubles."

"Explain?"

"The slain Hospitallers have been discovered."

"I expected nothing less. The men would have been missed when they failed to return. We have not the time to offer our allegiance in the avenging process. Later perhaps, when Jesmina is secure and the assassin's curse is lifted."

"No Miles, the St John knights do not seek our allegiance nor do they seek Saracen murderers. There are whispers of a bloody fight between Templars and Hospitallers. A fight witnessed by many at the arena."

"They blame us?"

"They will try."

"Who perpetuates such a myth? Not the desert dwellers or pilgrims who scattered as we fought. They would have seen, as we did, the true identity of the imposters as they shed their Hospitaller disguises."

"I fear the hand that poisons this cauldron may be known to us – to you."

Miles frowned. He knew of no one who would use the rivalry between the knights to this end. "Who?"

"Marchant."

"Guy-de-Marchant is long gone."

"Is he?"

Miles shook his head. There was no time to unravel this latest complication. "The Hospitallers must wait, and if they are directed in this madness by Guy, then he must also wait. The prince however cannot. We need Jesmina. Please tell me that she is safely secreted."

Thomas nodded. A smile twitched the corners of his mouth. "It appears the lady Jesmina holds many hot-blooded males in thrall, fearless knights and fearsome desert dwellers, but it has fallen to one little man barely old enough to wield a bow, let alone a sword, to protect this dusky maiden."

"Edmund?"

"Indeed."

Miles had been suspicious of Maleficius' provenance since their first encounter. Admittance to the covered wagon which served as the man's travelling abode did nothing to dispel his disquiet. The walls were draped in the finest silks, the floor thick with luxuriant fur. Above his head a celestial panorama had been exquisitely painted. The tiny lair could not have been more splendid had it been a baronial chamber, but the air was thick with a cloying scent that made it difficult to concentrate on the task at hand.

The magician puffed at his pipe and Miles squinted at him through the vapour. Edmund sat alongside, an infant monkey cradled in his lap. The boy had the sheepish look of a disloyal hound. Had he been in possession of a tail, it would have flicked with apprehension. In that moment Miles wondered how many times the lad had been beaten by his previous master and how much work still lay ahead to win the child's trust.

"Edmund, Thomas tells me that you keep the lady Jesmina safe while all around seek her out. Good lad. We need her now most urgently." The boy's pale face creased into a relieved smile and behind him a curtain twitched and Jesmina appeared.

"Miles." She acknowledged him with a dip of her head. The self assurance was gone. Fear had cast its shadow.

"You are well?" He supposed that hidden here among the misfits, Jesmina was safer than if she were surrounded by Templar swords, for both sides regarded the magician with a wary respect. Neither would imagine anyone of sound mind placing themselves willingly within his

121

clutches. Nevertheless, safe or not, the turn of events did not sit well with Miles. Maleficius, master of the bizarre and unnatural, was now, by default, controller of their destiny. He slid his gaze once more to the man and tried to second guess his motives. The man narrowed his red-rimmed eyes and snarled his broken smile.

"Thanks to my little knight Edmund, I am well," answered Jesmina. "And with *The Wondrous One's* help I hope to remain so."

"I see." Miles did not see. His mind was a jumble but he had not the luxury of time to allow for the sorting of such a muddle. "Jesmina, once again it seems I am in your debt, yet I must ask for one more indulgence on Hugh's behalf." He leaned close, an attempt to impart the urgency of the situation and to put himself between Jesmina and whatever malevolent influence the magician wielded. "Yesterday you were at pains to deliver a message. It went undelivered and I believe the assassination attempt on the future king is the result. What can you reveal about the assassin? Why does the prince's wound fester as if the devil himself wielded the knife?"

Jesmina looked to Maleficius and Miles felt anger begin to simmer. He longed to shout at her, to insist that she look only at him, that she answer only him. Instead he dropped his voice to a low whisper and leaned closer still so that his words reached her ears only and his breath caressed her skin.

"My lady, if not for the future king of England, then do this for Hugh. I know you hold him dear and today he is in desperate need of your council. If Edward dies under Hugh's care then the assassin's curse will have touched us all. If you care anything at all for the man you know as The Fox – help him. Please."

Jesmina placed her palm gently against his stubbled cheek. "You are a good man, Miles. Hugh is the better for knowing you and you will grow wiser from knowing him." She sighed softly. "My father is a weak man. He trades with the east wind in the morning, the west wind in the afternoon. He sees no folly in duplicity, merely business. Two days ago he made a sale of the deadliest poison from the most potent of snakes."

"The assassin?"

Jesmina nodded sharply. "The poison when applied to the sharpest blade will pierce the flesh and travel deep within the wound thwarting any attempt at healing."

Miles shook his head. This was not what he wanted to hear. "There must be a cure, a solution. There has to be."

"When applied promptly, yes. But there has been delay. I cannot guarantee that any antidote will be successful."

"But it could?"

"The wound must be cut away, pared back to living flesh, the tincture applied ..."

"And you have such a tincture?"

Once again Jesmina looked to Maleficius. Something indiscernible passed between them. Miles sensed the enormity of the gesture. The man blinked slowly and as his eyes re-opened he reached beneath his cloak and produced a small ampoule which he held up to the light of a flickering candle. He shook the glass vial gently and the opaque contents took on a strange luminescence.

"Poison?" Edmund scrambled backwards, his fearful whisper ignored by all as Miles reached out for the vial.

"Antidote?" Miles waited with outstretched palm, fascinated by the shimmering contents.

"Magic," cackled Maleficius. He held the prize just beyond reach and his lips twitched into an unholy grin.

"You wish to trade?" Miles could not believe the nerve of the man. He reached for the dagger at his belt and his hand was stayed by Jesmina.

"The trade is already done, Miles. Take the potion and go quickly. Have Hugh apply it to the open wound. The prince will live if your God wills it."

"And the trade?"

"As I said, it is done."

Miles looked from Jesmina to Maleficius and his stomach churned. He feared that Hugh would not approve. He certainly did not. "And all parties are in agreement?" he asked as he pocketed the vial and reached for the boy. He may, by necessity, be obliged to leave Jesmina behind, but he would not leave the child a moment longer in such a place.

Jesmina smiled sadly. "Go brave knight. Find your benefactor, save your prince." She reached out and tousled Edmund's hair as Miles pulled him roughly by the sleeve. "Someday if the Gods are willing, we shall meet again little man, and you shall be grown and I will be happy – and free."

It took until dusk for the potion to work its magic, for the antidote to nullify the ravages of Saladin's most deadly poison and reverse the fortunes of the future king. It took almost as long for the covetous courtiers and green-eyed physicians to stir their cauldrons and hatch their own insidious plots. As word of Hugh's success, threatened to leak beyond the royal appointments, those with most to lose leapt into action. The story of the mysterious soldier-surgeon, skilled tactician, invaluable peacemaker and trusted royal confidante' was twisted beyond recognition and instead, the impressionable of Acre were fed a far more agreeable tale. For it was whispered, on good authority, that the good lady Eleanor alone had saved her husband's life by sucking the poison from a wound gone bad.

As the sun rose above Acre, revengeful Hospitaller troops scoured the streets in search of Templar blood and Saracen spies lurked in the shadows in hopes of catching sight of the traitorous Jesmina. If ever there was an optimum time to leave Acre behind, this was it.

Maleficius loaded his menagerie aboard the last trading vessel and the ship lurched beneath the weight, the swell soaking many at the quayside. The sailors averted their eyes as men and creatures of the like that filled their hearts with dread, crammed into every available space. Like Noah and the magnificent Ark, Maleficius oversaw the embarkation with a steely eye and raised staff. The captain grumbled loudly at the delay, the tide would not wait forever, but not every passenger was aboard and he had already taken payment from a man he did not wish to cross.

Miles saddled his horse for a fight not a journey. Although he yearned to leave and put the heat of The Holy Land behind him, he had unfinished business in Acre. The Hospitallers were determined for revenge and it seemed no amount of peace-making by Hugh would appease them. Miles was certain that Guy was at the root of it.

"Miles, the men and I shall hold off the Hospitallers. Take the lad and head for the dock. The ship is almost ready to raise anchor." Hugh nudged his horse close while behind him among the remnants of the camp Edmund paused in his work, his pinched face hopeful.

"And leave the men to fight in my stead, I think not." Miles crossed to Edmund and hoisted him onto the pack-pony's back. "If Edmund's safety concerns you, take him yourself. Thomas and I will hold off the harbingers."

"My place is with the men, Miles. There is still a chance I can convince the St Johns' that they should be seeking Saracens rather than Templars."

Miles shook his head. He doubted that very much. The mischief makers had been hard at work and the whole city was fresh to the news of the terrible tragedy, the vicious slaughter, knight upon knight. "Hugh, for once your silver tongue will not help us. Marchant is behind this devilment. I am convinced of it and it is I who he seeks to punish with his lies. I shall stay and settle this once and for all. You take the men and board the ship. I shall join you before the tide turns."

125

"A noble, yet reckless offer, Miles, alas there is not room for us all. Maleficius and his elephant have seen to that. The good ship la Seynte Marie sits so low in the water the captain fears she will crawl on the sea bed all the way to Sicily." Hugh shook his head at the heavily laden pony as if that too would cause the ship to struggle further. "Seek out a Templar preceptory as soon as you reach Italy and deposit your loot, it's unwise to carry such trove."

"If there is not room on the deck, let the ship sail and we shall all take our leave on the next vessel. Another week, another month, what difference will it make?" Miles mounted, steadying his horse with a few chosen words. All around men readied for battle and the clatter of armour and weaponry echoed against the stone of Acre.

"I need you on that ship, Miles."

"Why?"

"To protect something valuable to me."

"Jesmina?"

Hugh grimaced. "Perhaps. She saved the prince. She put herself in jeopardy for you, Miles. You owe her your protection."

"She is with Maleficius, *The Wondrous One*. She has no need of impetuous knights. His *magic* will protect her."

"The journey is long and fraught with danger. She needs a champion who does not court devils."

"Exactly, and that man is you, Hugh."

Hugh shook his head. "I regret it is not, Miles. I have had cause to pass the devil on a dark night more times than I care to remember."

Miles snorted. "As have I, or have you forgotten?"

"No. I do not forget, and that is why I need you gone from this place. We are all on borrowed time, Miles. We cannot afford to waste a moment in argument."

"And what of Guy, you expect me to run from him like a whipped dog so I may play chaperone to a lady who dallies daily with men's hearts? I wager it is Maleficius who will need protection – from her."

126

"I expect you to follow orders," hissed Hugh. "Put Guy from your mind. There will be time enough for him you may be assured of that. The Hospitallers bar the quayside. They rally to prevent our escape, yet by some strange quirk of fate their presence simply protects the treasure Baybars seeks. La Seynte Marie will sail with Jesmina *and* you on board, Miles, and I'll hear no more argument from you."

Miles scowled his disagreement. "If the quayside is blocked how do you suppose Edmund and I will pass. Surely you do not expect Maleficius' sorcery to come to our aid."

"No I do not. In this matter aid will come solely by virtue of negotiation. My negotiation. Now for pity's sake, do as I ask. Take the boy and wait by the church of St John. A trusted man will meet you there. The men and I will create a diversion." Hugh reached out and gripped Miles' arm. "Miles, you must trust me. All will be well. We shall follow when the royal party vacate Acre. I dare not withdraw until then, there is too much at stake. Fear not, we will meet again, I know this."

"Where, where shall we meet?" Suddenly Miles was uncertain. He'd spent his formative years with this man who had guided him, bullied him, driven him mad at times with frustration, and the idea that they might never cast eyes on each other again filled him with dread.

Hugh smiled reassuringly. "Make your way back to Normandy. No doubt we shall catch up with you long before you reach my domain. Be cautious. Keep the lad close. Do not seek trouble or adventure along the way. Use Templar lodgings where possible and, Miles,"

"Yes,"

"Be safe."

Six

The streets were abnormally quiet, as if the citizens had been commanded to stay indoors, to bar their windows and look away. Miles drew his sword and urged his horse on. Behind, at the end of a short tether, the pony carried not only his possessions and spoils of war, but also the boy, Edmund. The child clutched his bow tightly, his pinched face both fearful and determined.

"All will be well," murmured Miles, using the same reassuring tone that Hugh had used with him, though inside his heart beat an unsteady rhythm. He could not understand why Hugh would send him into the very jaws of their enemy. The rival knights would not have left their fortress unguarded. "Hold fast, Edmund," he continued, "Hugh must have a plan for us."

As he approached The Knights Hall, the massive gate swung open. Miles gripped his sword more tightly edging his horse to the left so that his sword arm was unrestricted. Edmund raised his bow and tried to string an arrow with trembling fingers. The weapon slipped from his grasp and tumbled to the ground.

The Hospitaller who stepped out of the shadows to retrieve it was none other than Henri-de-Veloque. He paused a moment to consider the crudely fashioned arrow and then turned his attention to Miles.

"Veloque! What nonsense is this?" Miles yanked at the reins and swung his animal around. Either Hugh's co-conspirator had been betrayed and replaced, or there was greater trickery afoot. Veloque stood his ground, seemingly untroubled by the giant beast and its flailing hooves.

"Templar, it seems your benefactor wishes to make certain your escape. I wonder why?"

"I do not need the help of a Hospitaller," spat Miles. "You believe the word of half-wits and devils and have your men run us into the ground. We did not murder your knights."

"I know."

"You do? Then why...?"

Veloque shrugged. "Subterfuge, Templar. The Great and Wondrous Maleficius is not the only one who deals in shadows."

Miles lowered his sword and glanced back the way he had come. He could not make sense of it.

"Come," commanded Veloque. The tide is set to turn. Captain Serifino will not linger, no matter the size of purse." Veloque mounted his own horse and led them not in the direction of the harbour, but into the strangely empty stronghold.

Miles swung his gaze left and right. He had heard tales of the stronghold, of the grand architecture and the wealth, but all he saw were empty chambers and feral cats. "Where are your men?"

"They linger at the harbour. They have need of a fight. They hope to catch themselves a Templar or two."

"Yet you admit you know the truth, that we Templars are not responsible for the death of your knights. Why then do you not stop them? Rescind your orders and allow us free passage to the ship."

"I have my reasons."

"And you expect me to trust a man who *has reasons*?"

"No, I expect you to trust the man who sent you to me. If you do not, then by all means turn around and take your chances with the Saracens. I wager they are just as keen to get their hands on you as my men are. You did after all, steal the Sultan's woman."

"I did no such thing."

"My lord..." Edmund spurred his pony on and Miles, aware of the child's fear, shortened the tether so they rode side by side. Their hoof-beats echoed in the stone vaulted space and it was soon clear that their path descended sharply.

"What madness is this? We seek the port and yet you take us to the doorstep of the hell."

"How else do you imagine we move our supplies and our secrets when the streets of Acre are filled with Saracen spies and Templar buffoons?"

"A tunnel?"

"Indeed."

Miles could not deny the ingenuity of the hand-hewn tunnel. Little wonder the Hospitallers always seemed a step ahead. He was impressed, but still confused and increasingly reluctant to admit his interest. "Tell me, Veloque, why? Why do you involve yourself in this? We are nothing to you but Templar irritants?"

Veloque frowned. When he answered, he spoke slowly as if he chose his words with considerable care. "The Fox is a sly one, as I'm sure you're aware. Shrewd, and knowledgeable, a favour here, a favour there, and when one least expects it, all notes are called in and one concurs not because The Fox threatens, but because he asks. He asks now that you and the lad reach the ship safely. That I can do, but you must trust me."

"Trust..." Miles did not know who to trust, but as Veloque spurred his horse on he had no choice but to follow.

Hoof beats echoed in the confined subterranean space, Edmund clasped his hands over his ears as the sound was amplified to painful levels. Miles ignored the racket and measured out the tunnel in his head, trying to work out the route they travelled and where they might emerge. Three hundred strides of the giant horse, more or less, and the tunnel drew to its conclusion. Veloque pulled his horse up sharply just inside the exit and dismounted. He reached for Edmund and lifted him from the pony. "Dismount, Templar. Remove your armour and load it onto the pony. And make haste, the tide waits for neither man nor beast."

"Remove my armour, are you mad?"

"Not entirely, though some might argue that I have my moments. In this instance I am entirely sane. If you wish to reach the ship alive you must discard the additional weight. Remove your fine armour and weapons and load them onto the pony."

"I will not hand over my sword – to any man."

"Then you may use it to fight the fish that swim in the bay, or the sharks out at sea." Veloque turned sharply, impatience transforming his face into an ugly scowl. Edmund took a cautious step back. "Use your brain, Templar. I can pass through the Hospitallers who guard the dockside. You cannot. One word from me and they will stand aside. I shall lead your horses safely to the boarding and my men will assume I am merely delivering promised goods to Captain Serifino." He gestured to Edmund and the pony, "A cabin boy, a pack horse and a destrier that has seen better days. They will not question my actions."

"And you expect me to disarm, hand over everything I hold dear, so that you may put a blade through my heart and leave me to rot in your secret tunnel."

"No Templar. Although I am at pains to understand why, it seems you are destined for greater things. Your boy, your destrier and your treasure will travel under the safety of my sword, my word, my reputation. That I guarantee, to you and to The Fox."

"My boy, my horse and my treasure, I see – and what of me?"

Veloque smiled. "You, young knight, must swim."

Stripped down to his undergarments and with only his dagger for protection, Miles felt undeniably vulnerable. A voice in his head berated him for what in essence was an act of pure madness. He had handed over everything he owned to a man he did not know, a man who could be in league with Guy-de-Marchant for all he knew. If he had not seen Hugh in discourse with Veloque with his own eyes, he would not have put his faith in the man. All the same he decided to defer judgement on the matter until he was safely onboard ship.

The water was reassuringly warm. Even so Miles slipped into the depths reluctantly, his dagger tightly gripped. He swam silently out from the internal anchorage, seeking cover behind the various small crafts. All the while he checked the progress of Veloque as he rode apace along the approach to the dockside. He willed Edmund to look straight ahead and not draw attention to his position, but instead the child swivelled in the saddle, scouring the surface of the water, desperate for sight of him.

Angry shouts skimmed the water as the altercation at the harbour gates between Templar and Hospitaller escalated beyond insults. A skirmish, theatre to entertain the watching Saracens, he hoped nothing more, Miles was sure that Hugh would contain things sufficiently. He could not bear to think that any of his brothers might fall to a Hospitaller blade on his behalf.

Miles took a breath, ducked beneath the water and swam closer, anxious to see for himself what had transpired. He did not trust Veloque. When he re-emerged, Veloque, as promised, had passed easily through the first barrier, escorted safely by his own men. Edmund and the horses followed unhampered. Although somewhat appeased, Miles knew that was not the only obstacle they faced. Beyond the port, on the rocky outcrops that overlooked the shimmering waters, Baybars men also waited. Perhaps they planned to raid the ship when she left the safety of the harbour. Perhaps that was why Hugh wanted him aboard. First though he had to get there and that was where Veloque's ingenious plan fell apart.

Between the scattering of anchored fishing craft and the broad hull of la Seynte Marie lay a stretch of open water. There was no cover, no opportunity to duck behind a boat should Baybars men turn their beady eyes from the port to the water, and despite his prowess on the battlefield, Miles was not the most able swimmer. Raised in the Northumberland hills, he was more used to chilly boulder strewn rivers than the deep waters of the Mediterranean. The distance to the safety of the ship measured at least the length of the Hospitaller tunnel. He cursed and he waited. He would not make his move until Edmund was safely aboard.

Taking advantage of an empty fishing boat he reached up and took hold of a trailing net, anchoring himself for a moment and conserving his energy while he waited. He watched as Veloque, true to his word, delivered the boy into the care of Captain Serifino. The two chatted for a moment. As the Hospitaller handed over the reins to Miles' destrier, Veloque turned in his direction and smiled. Miles was not convinced at the sincerity of the gesture, particularly when Serifino immediately called for the anchor and sails to be raised and the great vessel eased away from the dockside.

For a moment Miles was stunned. Had Veloque deceived them all? Or was this all part of the plan? That he would connect with the ship as it set sail, out there in the bay. Miles stomach rolled. He could barely make the dock let alone swim unaided into open seas. He pushed off from the cover of the small vessel and began to strike out through the water. As his shoulder took the strain, over on the rocky outcrop someone noticed his bid for freedom. The man's cry was aimed at the Saracens who waited like buzzards by the shore. As one they raised their bows and unleashed their arrows.

The fighting knights, distracted by the Saracen's shouts, rushed to the dockside and both Hospitallers and Templars shouldered each other aside to see what had the heathens so incensed that they fired their weapons into the sea. On the shore, men ran to launch the small fishing craft while from the outcrops the arrows continued.

"There is a man in the water," yelled one Hospitaller as he leaned out over the water for a better view.

"I do not count his chances. The Saracens have good aim. They will skewer him before he reaches his goal."

Thomas shoved aside the harbingers, "Where, where is the man?"

"There do you see? He swims like a flounder."

Thomas squinted against the sunlight on the water. He could see nothing but empty water peppered with the hail of arrows. And then suddenly the swimmer broke the surface, rearing up to take a desperate breath and Thomas stepped back in alarm.

"He is ours," he yelled.

All around the arrows hitting the water disoriented Miles. He heard Thomas call and homed in on the familiar sound. He sucked in another desperate breath and dove beneath the waves once again. Through the clear water he could see the murky shape of the ship's hull. It turned into the wind and while it manoeuvred he was able to gain some headway. When next he broke the surface he heard his name clearly. Thomas and William freed from the debacle with the Hospitaller's were on the sea wall cheering him willing him on. On the ship, Edmund yelled encouragement and with some encouragement from Jesmina, the Captain lowered landing nets. If Miles could only swim a little further, hold out a little longer, he could reach the net and if he could reach the net, perhaps he would have the energy to scramble up it, to safety.

He took another breath, gulped seawater along with air and spluttered desperately. This time when he ducked beneath the waves he thrashed in panic and waves crashed over his head.

"Miles!"

"My lord!"

The desperate voices pulled him back, the arrows drove him on and when he thought that his lungs might burst and his shoulder tear open with the effort, his fingers found the rough twine of la Seynte Marie's landing net and he gripped it tightly. He shook sea water from his face and glanced up. The ship side loomed above him and he clung desperately for a moment. He had not the strength left for the climb. He closed his eyes and his fingers began to lose their hold. Was this Veloque's intent, or simply his own inabilities that were set to thwart him? He was jarred back to reality by rough hands. All around him men swarmed like ants at the honey. Maleficius' troupe of acrobats scaled the nets with ease, gripping him firmly, supporting him as he raised one hand above the other and made his way laboriously upwards. At the top the wizened dwarves with the strength of men twice their size hauled him over the rail to the safety of the deck. He landed in a soaking heap, chest heaving, limbs trembling with exertion. Jesmina wrapped a cloak around his shoulders and hugged him tight. Edmund dropped to his knees, his face pinched with fear, his eyes wet with tears.

Miles reached out and gripped the boy's arm reassuringly. Inside his stomach churned with relief. A warrior's death on the battlefield was one to contemplate with pride, but to lie on seabed for eternity was a fate that filled him with dread. He sent up a silent prayer thankful that he had avoided a watery grave. Rising with Jesmina and Edmund's help he steadied himself against the ship's rails. On the quayside the Templars cheered his appearance, but his eyes rested on only one. Hugh raised one hand in farewell and Miles echoed it. *Be safe*, Hugh had cautioned and Miles fully intended to take heed of those words, but that didn't mean that trouble would not court him. He was, after all, in the company of Maleficius *The Wondrous One* and the sultan's *stolen* woman. Miles doubted the coming weeks would be uneventful. He turned with a sigh and smiled at the boy.

"Well, Edmund, it appears our journey home has finally begun. I trust you are ready for adventure?"

"I am, my lord," replied the lad, his eyes wide. "I surely am."

"And what say you, Jesmina?"

Jesmina's lips twitched into an answering smile, "Of course, my lord. Adventure is most appealing."

"Good. Then God's speed to us all."

****

The Burning Boy
Novella Three

The Camp of the Enchanter, Gascony: 1273 AD

High above the awestruck crowds, Azim the feathered boy performs. But there are those who covet this strangely gifted *familiar*.

Fleeing Acre in the company of the enchanter Maleficius, Miles of Wildewood and young squire Edmund work their passage among the performing misfits and wild beasts. As outraged clergy call for the heretic's blood and old enemies hound Miles across the length and breadth of Christendom, a fiendish firestorm engulfs the cavalcade and Azim disappears. Miles is forced to put aside his suspicion of Maleficius as he seeks to secure the safe return of the *phoenix*. Miles must save the burning boy before his flame is extinguished forever.

One

The boy, dark as night and nimble as a feral cat, scurried barefoot along a rope stretched taut between two poles. His jaunty gait belied the height and danger. Midway, he paused to grin mischievously at those who gathered below. Encouraged by their applause, he offered a rakish bow, teetering precariously as the rope swung. It took a moment to correct his balance, but when once again secure, he cocked his head to the burly roustabout who hugged the shadows like a shroud. A pre-arranged signal, it resulted in a well-aimed nudge at one of the slender uprights. The subsequent ripple along the hawser pitched the boy sideways and for a second or two it seemed that he would surely fall. The crowd gasped and the boy responded accordingly, flapping the feathered arms of his costume and swaying like a drunken fool until once again he regained his poise.

For a lad no more than six summers he was unnaturally gifted, a definite benefit as he performed twenty feet or more from the ground. Rumour suggested he was the Enchanter's own child, a spawn of the devil himself, a strangely gifted *familiar*. Others within the travelling troupe whispered of a hideous spell resulting in a terrible forfeit; either way, the child was totally sightless, his eyes mere milky pools peering out from his inky black skin. It was a wonder indeed that he was able to perform at all, never mind with such skill. Regardless of his debateable parentage, Maleficius the Wondrous One had done the lad a favour in keeping him close, for in the world beyond the confines of the circus the boy would have surely earned his crust with a begging bowl, or perished in the attempt.

The act was as old as the rope itself, every faltering step practised to perfection, yet the onlookers were none the wiser and heartily applauded every trip and stumble. As the boy raised one foot and balanced one-legged, the crowd cheered all the more and even the boy's peers paused to watch.

Yet, despite the satisfaction of the majority, some in the crowd were not so readily entertained. Word of mouth had preceded the troupe and carried with it an exaggerated expectation. As Maleficius the Enchanter's bizarre cavalcade paved a trail through Italy and into France the tales had become ever more fanciful.

Mysterious monkey-men with whiskered faces and tails protruding from their velveteen clothes; fearsome fire-breathing giants, as tall as trees, who could burn down a barn or roast an ox at the magician's command; dwarves as small as swaddled babes with the temperament of ogres, and sleight of hand so accomplished and daring that the God-fearing crossed themselves, just in case. Indeed, there seemed no limit to the wondrous and terrifying entertainment. The peasants flocked to bear witness despite the risk to their immortal souls, while The Church simmered with disapproval.

Fuelled with such tales it seemed the antics of a child on a rope, no matter the risk to his scrawny neck, did little to assuage the appetite of the minority who yearned for darker deeds. As the boy continued his aerial acrobatics, a rumble of dissent originated at the rear of the audience and began an insidious dissemination throughout the crowd.

"Trickery," bellowed a rough voice. "The lad is no more blind than I."

"No, sir." A portly woman protested loudly, puffing out her ample cleavage indignantly. "Leave the lad, for he is skilled indeed. Sightless they say and sightless he be, no matter what you choose to believe."

"Where is the Enchanter?" yelled another. "We pay for magic and get naught but a stunted cabin boy. Any sailor can scale rigging without missing a step. Any bilge rat can scuttle along an anchor line to ship or shore. We shall grow old and take to our beds while the urchin grins from on high like a demented want-wit."

"He is as skilled as a bird," said the woman. "See, how he balances as if both feet were planted on God's good earth, see how he spreads his feathered wings. Hush thy noise, be patient and we may see him fly."

"Nay, fool," mocked a third dissenter, his voice spiced with cunning, his eyes dark with malcontent. "Do not mistake the child for an innocent in need of your succour and support. He is but a hooded crow, the hatchling of heretics, and possessor of the evil eye. Pray he does not turn his gaze upon you."

The woman flicked an anxious upward glance at the grinning boy. His eyes were closed, nevertheless she drew up the corners of her apron and shielded her face with the cloth. Her tormentor responded with a cackle.

"Fear not, mistress, your soul shall be saved if you follow my lead. A pox on the sorcerer's spawn, I say. Soon the fledgling shall plummet from his perch and be trodden underfoot."

As those closest to the unrest stepped nervously away, a hastily contrived drum roll recovered the crowd's wavering attention and a scorching lick of flame worried the lad along the rope, nipping at his heels like a dog at a stubborn sheep. Orange and purple sparks caught the rough fibres, flickering in the darkness, and the boy danced sprightly to avoid them. The musicians picked up the beat with whistle and drum, the audience roared their approval at this new peril, and unseen in the shadows a fire-breather, his face black with soot, took another swig of Maleficius' noxious potion and prepared another breath.

141

"May God have mercy upon your souls," the taller of the hooded interlopers barked at those who cheered. "You applaud the devil's work."

Those near enough to catch the heat of his rancid breath edged further away, anxious glances betraying their doubt, while some began to nod their agreement, crossing themselves fervently.

"Come away, fools," the ugly voice continued, "lest the crow-ling pecks out your eyes and the demon turns his fiery breath on your miserable heads. I wager he will roast a fool or two this night. Do you not hear the grinding of his teeth? He salivates for the weak-willed. Come away, I say."

From his vantage point in the shadows, Miles of Wildewood observed the rabble-rousers with growing concern. It was not unusual to meet with objectors. On several occasions permission to make camp had been denied, the cavalcade turned away at city walls by a suspicious and God-fearing populous. Undaunted, the company had simply moved on and trouble was avoided at the expense of empty bellies. Random hecklers were easily extracted from the crowd and swiftly dealt with, but Miles sensed that the developing unrest had a darker origin.

Although initially at pains to mingle with the locals, it was clear that the men who sought to incite the crowd were not from the surrounding farms or villages. Their cloaks, designed to conceal rather than protect, were not of peasant weave and with heads bowed conspiratorially, their whole demeanour suggested a cohesive and sinister motivation.

His thoughts immediately slid back to the debacle he had left behind in Acre. Surely the Hospitaller scoundrels could not have followed him so far? He dismissed the notion almost immediately. The Knights of St John had better things to do than chase one man and his half-grown squire-ling halfway across Christendom. They were far better served protecting their stronghold from Baybars' Saracen heathens.

Of course there were others with motive for such action; he had no doubt at that, for many within the troupe were fleeing discord in some shape or form. By unspoken agreement none in the company questioned their fellows and no one talked freely of their past, least of all him, but Miles knew that he trod a path with murderers, thieves and worse.

Forced to flee Acre aboard the trading vessel la Seynte Marie, his association with the company of misfits and miscreants had begun simply as a means to an end. As weeks turned into months; however, the situation had changed and the alliance of convenience had matured into something of mutual benefit. Miles of Wildewood, brave Templar, and defender of the future king had, by necessity, put aside his white tabard in favour of the dubious colours of Maleficius the Enchanter. Subsumed into this strange family of exotic beasts and performing oddities, Miles accepted that despite the accusations of heresy that dogged the troupe, he was safer from the consequences of his past, than he had ever been. Latterly though, a dark sense of foreboding had overwhelmed his thoughts and invaded his dreams. Uppermost in both, was his growing distrust of Maleficius.

Two

Jesmina materialised, spirit-like, from the shadows and slipped her arm through his, reaching up on tip-toe to sigh softly in his ear. "Why do you frown?" she asked. Miles wondered idly at her ability to move so silently, perhaps the rumours of her past role as a spy were not so far from the truth. "The boy will not fall, "she continued. "Azim is as agile as an Acre street-urchin and is blessed with little understanding of danger. He is a creature of the circus, born and bred. He knows no other life. As Maleficius' protégé he is well protected."

Miles scowled. Maleficius...always Maleficius, he was sick of hearing Jesmina sing the man's praise. It was perhaps significant that the *great enchanter* was notable by his absence. Normally at centre stage with his sweeping black cloak and hideous broken snarl, this night, instead, he lurked in shadows and whispered in the ears of men Miles neither recognised nor trusted. The Orientals had joined the troupe that morning and been closeted with the Enchanter for the entire day. It was clear they colluded in some dark plan for even Jesmina had been refused admission to their tryst. His suspicion of the man grew unabated. He could not ignore the feeling that Maleficius was party to a much larger game.

Jesmina, beautiful, cunning and cloaked in her own mystery was another whom he did not wholly trust, but for entirely different reasons. Her duplicity however was more subtle. She seemed determined in her mission to win him over, whether he desired it or not. He suspected he was

144

simply substitute for the man she really coveted. With no word from Hugh since Acre, it seemed Jesmina's patience was growing thin.

He wondered how long she had remained hidden within the shadows and whether she too had noticed the cloaked intruders. Perhaps they were in fact Jesmina's own enemies, sent by Sultan Baybars himself, to recover his property.

"My frown is reserved for other matters, Jesmina," he replied with a nod in the direction of the restless crowd. "In any event the Enchanter may do as he chooses with those who feed from his crumbs. The child, Azim, concerns me only in the event that he distracts Edmund from his duties." He focused on the huddle of gaudily garbed jesters and oddities awaiting their cue to the left of the high-wire. Edmund stood among them, entranced by the atmosphere, eyes raised in wonder at his small friend's skill.

"Oh, Miles. Edmund is joyous. Look, see how he smiles. Would you rather he spends his days in servitude, fetching and carrying for a spoiled knight? A knight who it seems does not appreciate a beautiful woman when he sees one." Jesmina fluttered her lashes in vain.

Servitude? Miles discounted her accusation with a snort. By comparison to the life Edmund had endured before being rescued, his current life was one to be envied. "You consider me spoiled?" he asked.

"I believe you contrive to achieve the outcome of your own choosing."

Miles shrugged. "Show me the man or *beautiful* woman who does not. But enough of me, let's discuss my young squire and the time he wastes playing with halfwits when he should be practising with the bow. One day soon he will have need of a steady arm and a good aim. His daily lessons prove to me his attention is elsewhere."

"*His* attention is elsewhere..."Jesmina expelled her frustration through pursed lips. "Those halfwits saved you

145

from a watery grave and have kept you and your boy fed these past months," she admonished sternly. "Let's not forget that, *brave* knight."

An apologetic smile saved Miles from further wrath, as he knew it would. It was a game they played daily. However his dissatisfaction with his present duties was no excuse to malign those who had proved to be good and faithful companions.

"I bow to your greater wisdom, Jesmina. They are without question an admirable fellowship and I include you in that, my lady." He raised her hand to his lips briefly and caught the angry flash in her eyes as she recognised the tease in his. "Be assured I am suitably chastened for my churlishness and will be ever grateful for our association. Nevertheless, Edmund has a job to do and at present I see little evidence of his endeavours."

He disentangled himself from the distraction of Jesmina's determined grip and moved her aside, all the better to continue his study of the incomers. Perhaps they were merely ale-fuelled opportunists come to pick the purses of the unwary, or hired men in the pay of disgruntled clergy. Miles smiled wryly at that thought. They would be surprised indeed to discover the enchanter was protected on his travels by a Templar. A tarnished one perhaps, yet a Templar nevertheless. But no, he sensed an alternate more devious motive for their arrival and it was time he discovered that purpose.

Jesmina sidled closer, following the object of his distraction with narrowed eyes. A sly smile twitched her lips. "You worry too much, Miles. Always you anticipate danger when there is none. Perhaps you crave the excitement, the taste of fear, only you may answer that, but we are far from Acre, from demons real and imagined. Can you not put aside thoughts of dark deeds and revenge and simply enjoy your time with us? I could make your stay far more enjoyable." Jesmina slid her arms around his neck and breathed her mischief at his ear.

146

"Behave," he murmured, as once again he disentangled himself from her grasp. Although sorely tempted he could not allow himself the undoubted pleasure of her company. He returned her pout with a heavy sigh. "I fear you confuse me with another, Jesmina. I protect your reputation as well as your skin."

"Pah," she snorted in reply. "The Fox has abandoned me....I am alone and in need of more than protection from my brave knight."

Miles smiled indulgently. The temptress was nothing if not persistent. "I am not *your* knight and Hugh has not abandoned you. I am here with you at his bidding, am I not? We missed our original rendezvous because Maleficius insisted on re-routing the ship to another port. We continue to miss pre-arranged meetings because Maleficius demands a change of course or extended rest stops. It seems The Great and Wondrous One has plans of his own to which we are not privy. Either way, I have no intention of taking Hugh's place in your affections – or your bed," he stooped to whisper in her ear, "no matter how tempting the prospect might be."

Despite the arduous journey and her current disadvantaged circumstance Jesmina's beauty and vitality were undiminished, a tonic indeed for a bruised soul, should he care to imbibe. However his loyalty to his mentor Hugh far outweighed any personal inclination. He wondered though whether her continued defence of Maleficius was linked to the bargain she'd entered into to save the life of the prince. Without her sacrifice, Edward would not now be king and for that he should be grateful. Yet he hoped that Maleficius had not claimed his prize. The thought of her with the hideously disfigured enchanter left him with a bitter taste.

"We are a family, are we not?" continued Jesmina, unabashed. She sought his hand, threading her slender fingers between his and encouraging him away from the distraction of the crowd. "We all seek the veil of obscurity.

147

The Wondrous One is a master of illusion. He has kept us from harm and will continue to do so... if you allow him. You misjudge him, Miles."

Miles was certain that he did not misjudge. Maleficius leached evil from every pore. Though, perhaps on this occasion Jesmina was correct and he worried needlessly. To date, both he and Edmund had remained safely concealed within Maleficius' ragtaggle troupe and the preceding weeks had given him no real cause for concern, but still his churning gut taunted him and the arrival of the mysterious cloaked intruders bothered him even more.

He pulled himself upright, away from her, the temptation of her alluring scent, and away from the wagon that shielded them both from view.

"A family you say? Then, my lady, I would ask that you utilise whatever maternal instincts you might possess and rescue Edmund from his idleness while I attend to those who threaten our domestic idyll. I believe the men who hide their faces are set to do us harm and it falls to me to discover what and why."

"Harm?" Jesmina exhaled her disbelief in a frustrated sigh. "You see, I am correct. Your desire for battle outweighs your common sense. There are no hooded assailants, merely a mob of awe-struck milkmaids and goat-herders. Do you fear a milk pail on your head?"

Miles threw a sly smile back at her. "You forget, Jesmina, your majestic stallion is highly prized by its *rightful* owner, as are you. I wager your new friend Maleficius is far too busy concocting his latest potion to protect either you or your horse from those with ill-intent."

He turned from her outrage and whistled sharply. Despite the din from the crowd the piercing note caught Edmund's attention. The boy turned, confusion quickly replaced by a fleeting guilty grimace.

The boy had settled easily into the bizarre ungodly company. A general dogsbody he toiled daily among the performing beasts, the miniature ponies and shackled monkeys, splitting his time between his duties as Miles' squire and his need to earn his keep within the troupe. While Miles admired Edmund's tenacity and willingness to prove himself, he viewed the lad's awe of Maleficius with distaste. It seemed the man had enchanted all but him.

"I wer only watchin' Azim," Edmund announced breathlessly as a shove from a disgruntled patron sent him sprawling at Miles' feet. An infant monkey, barely the size of a clenched fist, clung to his shoulder, its fingers furled in the loose weave of his jerkin, its tail wound tightly around its own trembling body.

Since making port in Sicily the tiny creature had shunned its own kind and chosen Edmund as its closest ally. The boy was a far more affable companion than the monkey's own bad-tempered kin and Miles had long since given up any attempt to separate the two. Edmund was convinced that the creature was a talisman sent to protect them from harm. Miles had yet to see the proof of that but in light of their current circumstances, and the lack of worthy relics, any additional protection could only be welcomed.

The monkey chattered its disapproval as Miles gripped Edmund by the scruff of the neck and hauled him to his feet.

"Watching Azim, when instead you should be keeping watch over the livestock. The crowd is rowdy, the animals are restless and all the while you gaze at the antics of Maleficius' performing pet, like a moonstruck hare." He shook his head, his censure half-hearted. He could understand the boy's attraction to the spectacle, even if he was irritated by it. He gestured to the monkey. "Your own little talisman may find himself skewered by hungry peasants and roasted over a hot flame if you are not more careful, Edmund." He had considered the option himself when food was short, but not for long. The beast was so small it was barely worth the effort to remove its skin. In

149

any event Edmund's outrage would certainly have soured the meal.

Edmund's face creased with concern and he shielded the creature with a grubby hand.

"You are too harsh, Miles. The child believes every word you utter." Jesmina scolded him with a shake of her head. "Dearest Edmund, ignore this evil knight. I fear he is in need of some entertainment of a wholly different kind to cheer his soul. Your tiny babe is quite safe." She reached out and gently stroked the creature's head, extending the caress to Edmund's cheek. "Run now, as your master commands and ensure that our trusty mounts are not distressed by the commotion. It is indeed a raucous evening."

Edmund smiled, his grin spreading even wider as Miles rolled his eyes at Jesmina's rebuke and cuffed the lad half-heartedly. "If Jesmina has her way you will be as soft as a maid by the time we reach English shores. On your way, Edmund, I entrust *Coquet's* safety to you, be certain not to let me down."

When the lad dispatched Miles returned his attention to the men who had raised his suspicions. He counted four. All similarly dressed, their faces purposefully obscured. They continued in their mischief, a word here and there, a shout to unsettle the gullible and as they bated and harangued, the masses were pressed ever closer together. He was keen to dispel any further unrest before it could spread and risk the evening's badly needed income. An uneasy crowd would not spend freely and after many months on the road Miles knew how finely Maleficius balanced his coffers.

"Why so suspicious? The crowd is merely boisterous this evening, too much wine or local brew perhaps?" Jesmina remained obstinately at his side, her hand on his arm, fingers caressing ever so slightly. "You do little to encourage their participation in the evening's entertainment when you glare at them like a common ruffian."

"Have you nothing better to do?" Miles muttered impatiently as he removed her hand. "Return to the safety of your wagon, Jesmina. There is something amiss here, whether you accept it or not, and I have no desire to drag you with me into the melee. Your good friend Maleficius would no doubt object should I return you in a state of disarray."

Jesmina's mouth shot open, her sharp retort prepared, but before she could deliver it, a shout erupted from those nearest to the show and all heads turned in that direction. This time the pole had suffered a far weightier nudge, the rope, now well alight, bucked like a whip and the boy's sure-footedness failed him. His artful tumble was accompanied by a collective gasp from the crowd, for it seemed the boy had emerged from within a halo of iridescent flames.

Still the child did not fall. Instead he caught the rope with practised hands and swung, monkey-like. As flames appeared to shoot from the plumes stitched to his sleeves, his feet dangled mere inches from the roof of a shrouded enclosure beneath him.

Miles suppressed a shudder at the sight. He had witnessed it many times before, knew the outcome did not merit his reaction, but on each occasion he found himself transported back to a time best forgotten, as if his conscience would not allow him rest from the horrors of his past. The image of the burning boy was ingrained and would not be shifted.

He ignored Jesmina's curiosity, her arched brow and open mouth, the words framed but unspoken, and instead flicked a suspicious glance back to the rabble-rousers. Despite the increased suspense in the ring the men continued to heckle, pushing forward through the crowd even more earnestly than before. The peasants stepped warily aside and as gaps appeared amid the mass, the visibility improved. Miles thought he glimpsed a flash of metal, an ill-concealed weapon perhaps, but he couldn't be sure. And equally couldn't decide on the motive for disrupting the entertainment. Who among the troupe was their target? Not the boy, surely. Could his own enemies have really followed him this far, or had the heretic Maleficius, acquired his own? Either way, he could not leave the matter unattended.

"To your wagon," he commanded Jesmina brusquely, as he withdrew his dagger and stepped into the melee.

Three

Not for the first time since leaving Acre, Miles regretted the unfortunate parting from his fellow knights. Together they were a force to be respected and feared. With Thomas Blackmore's astuteness and the wise counsel of his mentor Hugh-de-Reynard they shared an easy comradery. No task was insurmountable, no enemy too great. Alone, he had merely quick wits and recklessness at his disposal and when faced, as now, with men who brokered subterfuge he doubted his prowess on the battlefield or skill in the tournament would count for much.

He forced his way between the masses, ducking this way and that in an attempt to keep his prey within sight. It proved an impossible task. It seemed that no one wanted to miss the moment when the lad was either burnt to a crisp or plunged to an uncertain fate and men and women alike stood firm, all eyes raised to the spectacle above. An aged crone blocked his path spitting incoherent venom from a gaping toothless mouth, her drunken sot of a husband swayed and stumbled at her feet. Miles pushed her aside impatiently and stepped over the old man. He had no time for the ale-addled. A glimpse of black cloak drew him further into the crush while above his head the boy, Azim, continued to dangle.

As the boy held tight to the crowd's attention, the massive sail-cloth covering the enclosure beneath him was hauled aside. The audience and hecklers alike were immediately hushed. Inside the cage, a massive lion paced back and forth. Paws the size of babes heads, left craters in the soft earth as the frustrated beast prowled the boundary of its confines. The animal's scarred head swung side to side; pink tongue lolling from a cavernous gaping maw, while a rasping pant accompanied the occasional half-hearted roar.

Miles paused, as distracted as all the others by the boy's perilous plight. Soon others from Maleficius' troupe would appear to entertain the crowd, to draw their attention while the boy avoided the jaws of the aged lion and made his escape. It was simply a performance, a show that he had witnessed countless times and yet tonight there was an additional urgency to the proceedings, a frisson of danger in the air that tweaked at his subconscious. He tried to marshal his thoughts, to double check the pertinent details, but his wayward mind would not obey.

He turned his attention away from the burning rope and back to the crowd, confident that the boy would not fall, the lion would not pounce and the peasants and dim-witted who looked on in awe, would see no blood that night. The same, however, could not be said for those who sought to cause unrest. He tightened his grip on his dagger and scanned the spectators with a new resolve. Yet, where moments ago he had seen black-cloaked harbingers aplenty, now all he saw were the upturned faces of an expectant crowd. He swung around, cursing loudly. He was not mistaken. He had seen the intruders with his own eyes and now they were gone as if by magic. The dark one, Maleficius, must surely be at the root of this mischief.

Distracted once again by the crowd's noisy demands Miles turned and watched as Azim feigned a fall, hanging by one hand from the burning rope while the lion reached up a giant paw as if to swipe him. The crowd shrieked with cruel delight, and on cue a small battalion of armoured dwarves appeared, marching in a poorly co-ordinated manner, clanking miniature swords against oversized shields to thwart the dangerous beast. The lion, well fed

154

and quite bored with the nightly ritual, was easily corralled into a waiting wagon and Azim was finally able to release his grasp and drop directly into a large water filled barrel. He emerged moments later like an otter from the sea, skin glistening, water droplets clinging to his hair.

Miles exhaled a held breath and silently berated himself for his wavering conviction. Of course the lad would not perish. He was Maleficius' protégé after all. He pushed his way forcefully to the outer edge of the crowd, scanning right and left for any sign of the intruders. As the crowd surged forward, all that remained of the dissenters was a discarded robe. He retrieved it with a muttered curse. Just as he had thought, the material was far beyond the means of peasants, the fabric soft to the touch, the stitching fine and even. He held it to his nose, and caught the stink of sulphur just as movement in the vicinity of the caged beasts caught his eye.

A man made his way with great purpose between the assorted carts and wagons, pausing occasionally to look over his shoulder as if he feared that he had been observed. Without the benefit of torchlight it was difficult to make out the man's features but if his reluctance to be seen was any measure then it seemed likely to Miles that he was one of the rabble-rousers. He followed at a discreet distance conscience the remaining intruders were unaccounted for and he may well be drawn into a trap. He tightened his grip on his dagger and closed the distance between them. Behind, the spectacle continued and the racket from the crowd proved an unwelcome distraction. Miles tried to ignore it, his attention reserved only for his prey.

The intruder paused outside Jesmina's wagon, and Miles took advantage, moving stealthily until he was a mere pace behind. Now, he could see the bulk of the man, the bunched muscle beneath the leather jerkin and the lethal dagger at his waist. The man cocked his head and scented the air as if aware he was not alone. Fearing his footfall had announced his presence Miles paused, drew a silent breath and held it, convinced that his pounding heart must be audible above the din of the crowd. He waited as the man relaxed his position and leaned in toward the sackcloth which draped the vehicle's roof and sides. Inside the wagon, Jesmina hummed softly, a tune Miles recognised from his time in Acre. He willed her silent before the intruder could be enticed by the sultry feminine tone, but he wished in vain. The man raised his hand and grasped the wooden frame as if he meant to step aboard and enter.

Reaching out, Miles grabbed the intruder by the shoulder, spun him around and slammed him back against the wagon. The vehicle rocked beneath the weight of the two combatants. Jesmina's melody transformed into a startled squeal, but her cry of alarm went unanswered.

"Explain yourself," Miles grunted. His whole weight trapped his captive. The tip of his dagger pressed so forcefully against the intruder's throat that blood scored the skin. "Tell me what devilment you and your cohorts are about? Why do you spread discontent and kindle unrest? Why do you stalk the quarters of a defenceless woman in dead of night?"

"Questions - questions. Methinks you are out of condition, brother. Slow down and take a breath. You grunt like an over-worked ox, tell me you've not been wielding a plough since last we met?"

"Thomas?" Miles yanked the intruder's hood free and his fellow knight grinned back at him.

"Is this the way you greet a friend, a knee in the groin and a knife at the throat? Be thankful that I am too weary to retaliate or else you would find yourself face down in the dirt."

Relief coloured Miles' returning smile. "You cannot know how good it is to see you again, Thomas. You are a welcome sight for a beleaguered knight. I had begun to doubt I'd ever see your worthless hide, or hear your complaints again. What brings you here at this ungodly hour, and from where?"

"More questions. Unhand me and feed me, and I might explain."

Miles removed the blade from Thomas' throat and smoothed his collar. "All in good time, friend. The hour is late and although that in itself denotes the urgency of your visit, I have my own matters of concern to attend to." He cast a quick glance over his shoulder, conscious that by following the wrong man he had allowed the intruders to go about their business.

Thomas wiped the blood from his throat with the back of his hand. "Food, Miles. Take pity for heaven's sake, I'm all but starved."

"Thomas you think of naught but your belly – as usual."

"With good cause. I've ridden nonstop from that bastard Gaston-de-Bearn's stronghold in the Pyrenees. If you want an account then you shall have it, but first I must find vittals, a bed and a willing maid to share it."

"Food and a bed I can provide, but as for a maid, I fear there is little choice here. Maleficius either enchants them for his own purposes or scares them away."

"What of the lovely Jesmina?"

Miles scowled, pulling Thomas away from the wagon and the earshot of the lady in question. "The lovely Jesmina is a wily vixen. I do not recommend you go there. In any event she pines for Hugh." He stepped away and scanned the shadows, realisation that Thomas was alone, causing him to falter. "Where is our leader?"

"Hugh? He remains with the king."

News of King Henry's death and Edward's ascension to the throne had been slow to reach the cavalcade as it journeyed first by ship then in a ragged lurching procession through Italy and onward to France.

"The king is dead. Long live the king," muttered Miles half-heartedly. His relationship with the new monarch was complicated. He was reluctant to renew his acquaintance lest it result in yet another mission to test his morals.

Thomas paused to study him momentarily, concern furrowing his brow. "Long live the king," he agreed "let there be no doubt about that, Miles."

"Of course. Like you, I am sworn to defend the monarch."

"Good. I'm glad you have not lost focus, or loyalty, Miles. Your assistance might yet be needed. The fool Gaston refused to present himself to the new Duke of Gascony and Edward will not let it lie."

"He is fully recovered?"

"Edward? As strong as an ox. He lays siege to the blaggard's stronghold and wines and dines in full view while Gaston and his household salivate."

"And what does Hugh think of this tactic?" Miles asked as he propelled Thomas away from the wagons and toward the camp that he and Edmund had set up away from the arena. The noise from the crowd was still loud and Miles was distracted by it. There was still the matter of the hooded interlopers to deal with.

"Hugh seeks a swifter solution," continued Thomas. "He has pressing business in Normandy, but Edward is in no hurry to return to England. The crown is secure and he wishes to attend appropriately to those who do not show due deference. He wishes Gaston to be dealt with as an example to others who think Philip of France the higher authority."

Miles smiled. "I fear you spend too long at Hugh's side, you spout politic like a true scholar."

"Nay, I simply relay a message. Hugh reads the situation and believes the solution may lie elsewhere."

"With me?"

"Perhaps, though that is not the reason for my heroic journey through the most terrible terrain." He affected a great sigh. "The peasants here about are as superstitious as a monk on mead, they jibber and wail at first sight of a stranger. My patience has been sorely tested. Thank the Lord for a swift horse and the strength of will to ignore the plaintive call of an empty belly."

"Thomas, much more of that performance and Maleficius will be offering you employment alongside the jesters. There will be work aplenty I can assure you, just listen to the applause of the crowd. It seems we have come full circle this night."

"Full circle?"

Miles gestured to the torch-lit arena. "The audience veer between rapture and ridicule. This night they are stoked half to madness and I have yet to ascertain the cause. But no matter, I have already assured you food, drink and a warm bed by the fire. You need not convince me further. Just tell me, what does Hugh need from me?"

Thomas sobered immediately. "Guy-de-Marchant is abroad once more, making trouble, whispering and plotting. He seeks you still with a greater will than before, if that is possible. Hugh believes he intends to intercept you between here and Normandy. Guy has spies and turncoats everywhere and Maleficius' antics have brought unwelcome attention to the troupe. It has been an easy matter for your enemy to observe your progress from afar and choose his moment to intercede. Hugh suggests that you take your leave of this cavalcade and make swiftly for the coast."

Miles cast a sharp glance around the darkened camp. He had not imagined the intruders after all. But if the men were in the employ of Guy, why had they not simply attacked? It made no sense.

"You wish me to run?"

"Hugh wishes it, not I, though I would caution you to heed his words. He is most insistent that you complete your journey home. There is no good served by having you slain by the hand of a coward such as Marchant."

"You assume that I would fall and he would not. Thank you for your vote of confidence, Thomas. And the situation with Gaston, how does Hugh expect to resolve the matter without our assistance?"

Thomas shrugged. "In truth I believe all help is needed if we are to get the king to England before the winter is upon us. If this siege does not resolve soon he shall suffer a defeat of the worst kind."

"Defeat?"

"Political embarrassment. Hugh the great arbitrator is sorely tested running in circles trying to find a solution that will appease both sides. Edward may well be Duke of Gascony and Aquitaine but Philip is still King of France and it would not bode well for our newly crowned king to be undermined by Philip's intervention."

"Hugh gives sound advice, Edward knows this. He has relied upon him countless times. Why should this occasion be any different?"

"The incident in Acre has soured Hugh in the eyes of The Church and they hover by Edward's shoulder whispering in his ear."

"He saved the life of the future king?"

"Nay, he colluded with a heretic to save the life of the future king."

"Maleficius?"

"The Knights of St John, have been oiling the wheels of suspicion. They are not yet avenged for their loss in Acre."

Miles snorted. "Baybars' doing not ours and Henri-de-Veloque knows this."

"What do you know of Veloque?" asked Thomas, his eyes narrowed with cautious interest.

"Enough." Miles shook his head dismissively, unwilling to reveal Hugh's alliance with the Hospitaller commander. It was not his story to tell. "Another time, Thomas, or we will tie ourselves up in the knots of our enemies' subterfuge. I fear we have enough of our own to contend with – don't you?"

"Yes, well the seeds of artifice flourish within the royal court and the sooner we are all free of it the better."

"You have another plan?"

Thomas grinned. "A slight diversion from your quest, it should not overly delay you and I sense that you grow bored with your present role."

Thomas was quite astute in that regard, already Miles began to feel anticipation for this new adventure. He gave another quick glance over his shoulder before stepping closer.

"Go on."

"A simple ploy, draw Guy and his harbingers away from your new friends and in doing so assist both Hugh and Edward. It does not hurt to have another good deed listed by the king and in doing so you might yet see an end to Marchant."

Miles frowned. There was danger involved in any covert mission carried out for the king, he wore the weight of such favours like a horsehair shirt, and it chaffed him daily. In truth he wished to be as far away from the king as possible, but if Guy was determined to force a final conflict before they crossed the channel, he could do worse than join his comrades in curtailing the siege. The thought of taunting Guy further with his apparent indifference to the threat, appealed to him. He would have his day of reckoning with his nemesis, but on a day of his own choosing.

Four

A shrill cry of alarm stilled Miles' response. "Fire!"Slicing through the encampment, it pierced the raucous din like a well honed blade. That one word injecting more dread into those still gathered, than any threat from hooded hecklers. Miles stiffened, one restraining hand gripped Thomas' arm as both men swung around in a bid to determine the direction of the alarm. In the same moment the audience also turned, mouths agape, cheers instantly silenced by confusion and fear.

Before the cry was fully formed the night sky was illuminated by an explosion so mighty, a ball of flame so bright, that the crowd bowed their heads and covered their eyes with frantic hands. It seemed the devil himself had risen up to smite them all. Torn timber shot skyward as carts and wagons were reduced to kindling in a single terrifying blast. Dismembered splinters the length of a sword and just as deadly speared the unwary, sparks showered like sulphurous rain, and as each fell to earth, a rainbow of flames erupted. Purple on the straw where bellowing animals rested, green on tinder-dry wagons and fiery red upon the heads of fleeing men.

All around, the screams of man and beast split the air. The frantic noise amplified by the close confines of the mob. In desperation the terrified crowd stampeded, running this way and that, trampling the old and addled underfoot, their direction driven and diverted repeatedly as new fire-bolts exploded ahead and behind. Animal trainers scrambled to reach their charges as cages were upended and beasts driven wild with fear were unleashed to run amok.

For a blink of an eye Miles remained immobile. It seemed his darkest nightmare had made the journey from night to day and he was powerless to repel it. Deep inside his gut, the parasitic seeds of guilt and betrayal continued their relentless fermentation. He was surely cursed.

"Edmund!" his voice exploded, propelled by the weight of fear pent up within. He'd sent the boy to tend to the horses, commanded him, in fact. Now as he stared in horror at the inferno he hoped he had not sent him to his death.

No he prayed silently, *please, God, not again. I cannot bear it. Take me if you must, but not the boy.*

"Jesmina?" Thomas bawled in his ear, yanking desperately at his sleeve. "Where is Jesmina?"

Miles hesitated, confusion slowed his reaction and in frustration Thomas tightened his grip, shaking him so roughly that he would have fallen were it not for his friend's determination to keep him on his feet.

"Miles, concentrate. We have only moments before the entire camp is consumed. Where is the lady Jesmina?"

"Jesmina..." Miles rolled her name around in his mind repeatedly as if that alone would hasten her appearance. When it did not, he turned to the spot he and Thomas had left only moments before. Many of the carts were already alight. Those that had so far escaped the flames were being dragged clear in a heroic bid to staunch the path of the fire. The scene however was one of chaos and uncoordinated actions, with carts colliding and men falling beneath the wheels or simply running for their lives. Unable to see beyond the heavy shroud of noxious smoke, Miles could only hope that Jesmina's vehicle had been spared.

"In the wagon where we came upon each other, she rests there... away from the melee." Miles shook his head at the absurdity of his own statement. If he had considered the camp in turmoil before, then he had no words to describe the chaos now.

"The melody – that was her. I knew it." Thomas' smile was fleeting as if the memory was spoiled by the thought that he may never hear her voice again.

"We must save her..." continued Miles, his voice trailing off as he frantically sought a solution. Jesmina was yet another innocent whom he had unwittingly commanded into the path of the inferno, and another who may perish as a result. Suddenly Miles the impulsive, decisive knight was beset with indecision. Jesmina and Edmund were both in peril, but he could not attend to both.

Horses straining madly at their tethers were suddenly freed and both men were forced to leap aside as the crazed animals turned from the flames and galloped directly toward them, eyes red rimmed, nostrils flaring. The noise of equine fear was relentless, loud and painful in Miles' head. He could not judge which was worse, the terror of man or beast. He stumbled, tasted dirt as his face hit the ground and despite the pounding hooves all around him, managed to right himself as the last horse careered past.

Spurred on by the cloaked harbingers, the animals scattered all those in their path. In their wake they left a trail of yet more sparks and burning embers as torches held aloft were discarded and the intruder's escape into the darkness beyond the firestorm assured. *Guy?* Miles could not be sure; such was the chaos all around him, but he could not discount it.

Forced apart by the swell of the fleeing crowd, Miles was separated from Thomas and unable to battle through the mass to reach the enclave of wagons. It seemed the decision over who to save was no longer his to make. He yelled to Thomas. "Find Jesmina and pray to God her wagon has not yet become a torch. I shall seek Edmund. The lad is somewhere in the thick of things. I cannot abandon him."

Thomas raised a hand in agreement. Across the heads of the writhing mass, and through the shroud of stinging smoke, the concern etched on his face, was obvious. "Take care, Miles," he called, "If the wind changes the hellfire shall consume us all."

Like flotsam caught by a retreating tide, Miles was swept further from his goal by the fleeing mob. He anchored his feet with some determination, grabbed the person nearest to him and bellowed in the man's ear.

"Water! We must have water if we are to withstand this." He snatched up a discarded pail, forced it into the man's hand and pointed at the giant barrel where the boy Azim had sought shelter. "Form a line. We must get water on those flames before the entire cavalcade is reduced to ash."

The man, wide-eyed with fear, but desperate for direction, nodded his understanding and word spread as quickly as the flames. Soon the dwarves, giants and performing oddities were unified in purpose. A great chain snaked from the barrel and when the contents were exhausted, the lumbering elephant was encouraged by its trainer to syphon vast gulps of precious water from the adjacent river and dampen the embers with its cargo. It could not be persuaded near the heart of the fire where flames leapt as tall the beast itself, here instead, the little men with giant hearts braved the heat and noxious fumes to quell the inferno.

"What shall I do?" wailed a man blackened with soot. He clung bravely to the tether of the muzzled bear. The animal roared with fright, dragging the man behind it like a bundle of wet rags. "I cannot hold him alone. Help me. I beg of you," he pleaded to any who would listen.

"A pox on the bear, leave him to his fate, we shall all be burned alive," called another as he stumbled past, a squealing piglet held tight under one arm. "Run. Run, while you can."

Miles grabbed the man by the scruff of the neck and threw him toward the tether.

"Grab hold and assist for pity's sake, or so help me I'll tie you to a stake myself." He caught at others who sought to save their own skin and thrust them towards tasks that required immediate attention, and only when assured that all knew their purpose and were busily occupied at it, did Miles resume his search for his squire.

"Edmund!" His voice hit a wall of smoke, the desperation in the single word immediately deadened by the pall. The lad could be within arm's reach and yet be lost. His gut twisted. He could think of no greater horror than that of the flame. "Edmund lad, if you value your hide show yourself now."

He dampened a cloth, and held it tightly across his mouth and nose as he trod a careful path through smouldering straw and burning embers. To his left the enclosure where earlier the lion had paraded, was now well alight, the sailcloth curling up into itself, the grease used for waterproofing dripped molten and unforgiving. Miles twisted away as the material ripped free from its tethering and flapped so close that the grease glanced his arm. He cursed aloud, his skin boiled but the intense pain merely helped to direct his focus.

"Edmund!" he yelled again. "For pity's sake boy, if you do not show yourself now I'll ..." His eyes stung, his throat was raw from shouting. His chest heaved with the effort of extracting what little oxygen remained. He dropped to his hands and knees in a desperate attempt to find breathable air so he might continue his search, and as he felt around in the charred remains, his hand came upon a small smouldering body.

Five

Miles burst into the enchanter's wagon, slamming the door back on its hinges. Pots and potions crashed to the floor and timbers groaned as he crossed the small lair in one heavy step. His right hand was raised in a tight fist, the charred and twisted remains of Edmund's monkey hanging rigid from it. Only moments before, with no sign of Edmund, he'd struggled to hold his composure. Now an ice-cold animosity drenched him from head to foot. If the lad were lost at the enchanter's hand, then the man would live his last moments in full regret.

Maleficius sat cross-legged, his angular limbs jutting out awkwardly beneath his robe. His eyes were closed as if in sleep or trance. The pungent scent of opiate suggested the latter. Mile face twisted into an angry scowl.

"Wake up, sorcerer. The camp is ablaze, the wild beasts run free to kill and maim. The witless run in circles and here you sit oblivious. You have lost it all, everything, including your mind so it seems. Does that not alarm you?"

Maleficius' hooded lids flicked open to reveal golden eyes, glazed with the sheen of confusion. He blinked slowly, as if to collect his thoughts before arching one black brow in enquiry. "Close the door, knight," he hissed.

Miles gaped at him. "Hell has come a calling, flames threaten you still, and you ask for a closed door. Do you worry that your knotted beard will take light or that the devil may reach in his hand and pull you back to

167

purgatory. Methinks you hide from the consequences of your own actions."

Maleficius exhaled. His breath exited his body like the last gasp from a dying man. "You seek to avoid the truth by accusing another, an expected reaction from a knight who buckles beneath the weight of his own guilt."

Guilt? The man had no concept at how much guilt Miles carried. While he prayed that he was not complicit in the evening's mayhem by virtue of his association with Guy, it did not take a stretch of the imagination to lay the blame for such a catastrophe at Maleficius' door. Marchant could not have orchestrated such a firestorm alone.

Miles glanced from the pitiful blackened creature in his hand, to the vivid burns on his own forearm and allowed the pain from the wound to sharpen his focus. He did not believe the man's ignorance of events, yet there was no gain to be had by bludgeoning the truth from him, even if it would satisfy his own keen desire for blood. He gripped the hilt of his dagger tightly instead. The mere thought of plunging it between the magician's ribs was solace of sorts.

He inhaled slowly, the heady mix in the small space was no worse than the smoke outside, yet the unusual pungency made his head swim. He reached out and steadied himself against the doorframe. The wood was intact and almost soothing to the touch. The fact that the enchanter's wagon had remained unscathed when all around had not, gave him cause to wonder more deeply at the man's involvement in the turn of events. He narrowed his eyes suspiciously.

"On the matter of truth, tell me, how is it that while all around is set to flame, you alone escape? Not a scorch, not a flicker has touched your wagon. What trickery is that?"

Maleficius shrugged his gaunt shoulders. "How do you imagine the burning boy survives the heat of the flame?"

The image of the child, haloed by fire, slid into Miles' mind, unbidden. He pictured the boy's small arms raised in defiance, the blue-black feathers stitched to his sleeves reflecting the menace of the picture. Miles could not prevent the resulting shudder. "Sorcery?" he hissed.

"If you wish. I prefer to call it knowledge," replied the magician, "and I seek knowledge everywhere and from everyone. You should follow my lead, knight, one day it may very well save your soul."

Miles scowled. "Tell me there is no connection between your clandestine meeting this evening and the cloaked hecklers who cause our patrons to mutter in alarm."

"*Our* patrons? Do not get above yourself, Templar. You are a mercenary, nothing more. Paid for your sword not your intellect. You no longer have the Fox to argue your corner nor watch your back."

"I have no need for another to watch my back. I am well able to see to my own defence and those around me if they so wish it. *You* asked for my protection, Maleficius, I provided it. All the way from Sicily, I have paid my way in the protection of this company of misfits and spinner of spells. But this night you test my patience and I tell you now, our paths have reached a crossroads, and I shall leave you to your fate, make no mistake."

Maleficius shrugged his contempt. "Indeed, the brave and fearless knight. Our saviour from the ruffians and purse snatchers who lie in wait by roadside and darkened alley, and yet is it not you, Miles of Wildewood, who hides behind the skirts of women," he smirked his black sharp toothed smile, "Tell me you are not attracted to the Sultan's whore, tell me that you do not secretly desire her."

Miles grimaced. "Do not use Jesmina to obscure the truth of this night or to deflect your own guilt in this matter."

"My guilt?"

"Your enemies stalk us like wolves at the scent of a lamb."

169

"And you have none? Why else are you here, Miles, among the misfits and maligned if not to hide from a nemesis who shadows your footsteps like a hound at a hart. Tell me, Miles, who dragged you aboard la Seynte Marie when the sharks would have torn the flesh from your bones. Who keeps you and your boy hidden despite the danger of reprisal? The Fox is right to shake his head at your impulsiveness. You bite the hand that feeds you, and covet his woman at the same time. A chivalrous knight indeed."

"I have more than paid my way," countered Miles. "Have I not warned you time and time again throughout our journey that there are those who would see you dead and see us all hanged for our association with you."

"I could argue that the same be applied to our association with you, Miles. You drag enemies in your wake like the smell of death from a grave."

Miles scowled. He did not need the reminder. He glanced back through the open doorway, he would surely know if Guy was near. He felt certain he would sense his enemy's presence, and yet he did not.

"Would you have me believe that you know nothing of the hooded dissenters who disrupted the evening's entertainment?"

"I do not concern myself with ignorant malcontents; the world is full of such fools. They bemoan their miserable existence yet do nothing to improve it. It is your job to deal with the unenlightened – is it not? The great Crusader, upholder of the Christian faith, if you have failed, then berate yourself, not I."

"Despite the efforts of the *unenlightened* the show continued, your misfits did you proud, Maleficius. Fear or thrall? Only you know the reason why they follow you so devoutly. Even the feathered boy continued to dance the burning rope, while calls of *heresy* abound. His blindness an unholy advantage for he fails to see the disquiet he generates in others and the subsequent risk it brings to all."

"Azim? Where is the boy?" A sudden flicker of alarm narrowed Maleficius' eyes. He dragged himself to his feet, limbs unfurling like a giant locust until he stood a good head taller than Miles, stooped within the confined space. Miles edged away, uneasy in such close proximity to a man whose provenance was questionable at best.

"Do you not listen? The fire has resulted in chaos. The boy could be trampled underfoot or burned to a cinder, as could Edmund. Do you not hear the commotion? Your wagons burn, your performing beasts escape the carnage due only to the courage of your troupe. Some were not so fortunate." He held the charred remains aloft. Maleficius wrinkled his nose distastefully and a jumble of incoherent words spilled out between his disfigured lips. Perhaps he too had considered the beast a luck-bringer and was at pains to counter any ill-fortune that might result from its untimely demise. "For pity's sake what is this madness?" continued Miles, "What have you done? Are you privy to the purpose of these intruders or must I turn this camp on its head in pursuit of the truth?"

"I suggest you look closer to home." Maleficius snarled, his sharp teeth glinting as he spoke.

Miles glowered back. "The men do not shout my name. They shout of heresy, of dark deeds. It is you, not I who incites their fury."

Maleficius raised a dismissive hand. "You look in dark corners for answers but begrudge the candle wax."

Miles stood fast, his patience fast expiring. "I have no time for your riddles, Enchanter. The men must be here at someone's behest."

"Indeed."

"You know as well as I do, this evening was simply a makeshift affair pulled together to bring in enough to feed the collective for another day. You, yourself gave the majority of the troupe a day of rest and if the stench in here is anything to go by, it would appear you have already taken your pleasure."

Maleficius began to rummage through various pots, his attention seemingly elsewhere as he chose, and discarded at will, receptacles labelled in unfamiliar cipher. His agitation escalated as the object he sought eluded him. His eyes darted back and forth but Miles knew that despite this obvious distraction, he still listened.

"One must assume the intruders had sense enough to count heads and draw their own conclusion as to the minimal size of purse."

Maleficius looked up sharply and Miles read the calculation in the man's eyes. Of course the magician had further funds secreted somewhere in the wagon, he would be a fool if he did not. Miles recalled Hugh's advice before they parted in Acre. He had been insistent that Miles deposit his own crusader spoils in the first Templar preceptory he came upon. It was advice he had chosen to ignore. His muttered curse was met with Maleficius' amusement.

"I wager you have more reason to worry about purse snatchers than I. Look to your own kind, Templar, before you cast your aspersions. You claim to offer protection but in reality you drag harbingers in your wake. You will not be rid of them until you rid yourself of whatever you carry, deep in your gut and heavy in your heart." He tapped at his chest. "You are the bringer of darkness not I. I suffer you because of a debt to The Fox. Reynard suffers you for reasons known only to himself."

Miles knew the enchanter's dire warning was simply a device to divert his attention from the truth. He had journeyed too far in the company of the strange and other-worldly to see it for anything else. Perhaps the sight of the burning boy had addled his wits somewhat. Nonetheless, while the fate of his young squire hung in the balance, he must retain control. He took a shallow breath and turned back to Maleficius his resolve renewed.

"I saw you earlier in deepest discourse with men who are strangers to this camp. What did you discuss?"

"Business, Templar. My business."

"It is my business if it has led to this." He gestured with frustration to the commotion beyond the wagon. "I cannot waste another moment in this endless debate. It is matterless who perpetrated this catastrophe, what matters, is that we are all still at risk by persons unknown and whether you wish it or not I will discover the truth."

He took one more step and it brought him face to face with the Enchanter. He raised his dagger until the tip rested at Maleficius' throat. "My squire Edmund is missing. If he is lost to the fire, you will wish that you too had burned in hell, for I'll not rest until I avenge him."

"Miles!" Thomas' low growl stilled his arm. The knight stood framed in the doorway. A warning scowl creased his brow. Jesmina clung to his arm, her hair askew, her clothes marked with soot.

"The boy is lost, Thomas. This dark one must pay."

"No!" Jesmina pushed forward. "This is not the answer, Miles. Do you not see? Maleficius can help us."

"Help? I wager he has done enough."

"Listen to her," said Thomas. "Why would Maleficius set fire to his own cavalcade, his caravan, his beasts, his people? It makes no sense. You wish to lay blame at someone's feet, so that you may exact revenge. I understand that and share your desire, but I fear you attack the wrong person."

Miles shook his head. "I don't have time to listen to this endless debate. Edmund may lie injured somewhere out there among the embers. He needs our assistance, not the benefit of our argument. The enchanter must await his fate. Be assured I shall return to deliver it in person." He made to push past Jesmina but Thomas' words were already sowing seeds of doubt in his mind. The fire made no sense at all. Reluctantly he turned back to Maleficius.

"In all my time in your company I have seen nothing resembling the horror of this night." Maleficius' eyes narrowed and Miles pressed on regardless. "You summon flames at will. You use them in your act. The burning boy, the fire eaters... Who, other than you, could create such a spectacle? Who would dare? If this was not a deliberate act, then what, an accident, some alchemy gone wrong? Tell me, magician, I give you fair chance now to explain."

Thomas reached out and caught Miles by the arm. A hefty tug pulled him away from Maleficius and out of the wagon. "Leave it, man. Put aside your suspicions, Edmund did not perish in the fire. He is nowhere to be seen. I have scoured the encampment. The boy is missing and so are your horses."

Maleficius hovered at the open door, his hawk eyes flitting from one burned wagon to another. The flames were all but extinguished yet the horror remained, curling in smoky tendrils.

"Missing you say?"

"Lost, enchanter, and I lay the blame squarely at your door."

"And Azim, also?"

"Azim? I care not for your performing pet, Maleficius. I seek only my boy."

"Then you are a bigger fool than I imagined, knight. You do not see treasure when it is placed in your hand, whereas others covet it greatly."

"Treasure?" Thomas cocked his head. "Is that what this is all about, gold?"

"Treasure has many forms." Maleficius withdrew a jar from his collection of many and threw it into the air. It spun on its upward trajectory and then dropped like a stone, directly into Thomas' outstretched hand. Disappointment twisted Thomas' face into a scowl when in place of the expected precious contents, the jar revealed merely a pungency guaranteed to repel the most inquisitive treasure seeker. "Keep it, Templar, you may have use of the tincture to cover the stench of the inglorious road you travel."

Maleficius turned back to Miles, crooking his finger to draw him close and despite his revulsion of the man, Miles could not resist.

"Azim will have the answer to your boy's whereabouts." The timbre of the enchanter's voice stilled Miles' caustic response. The man was deadly serious and for once there was no hint of theatre. He did not appear unduly troubled by the loss of his wagons, but the disappearance of the burning boy obviously bothered him greatly. "Find my little phoenix and you shall find your squire. Return the phoenix safely to me and I will provide the answers you seek. But take heed, Templar. Extinguish the flame of the burning boy at your peril. He is the seer and through him your destiny will be revealed."

Six

The men made their way through the charred encampment, Jesmina, close at heel struggled to match their lengthy stride. All around, the soot-blackened and shocked troupe attempted some semblance of order, damping down the last stubborn embers, recovering what they could from the ashes.

"Have you seen the boy?" Miles questioned everyone. Grabbing their sleeve when they failed to hear, shaking them vigourously when they did not listen. "My squire, Edmund, have you laid eyes on him? Or Azim, have you seen the feathered child since the fire?" In the main he was met with vacant stares, such was the shock that resonated throughout the travelling folk. Those that retained their wits merely shook their heads. They had seen no children and were disinclined to help with the search.

"Leave it, Miles," said Thomas. "They have lost their livelihood. They will struggle to feed their own. They have no care left for your stable boy."

"There must be someone who witnessed their departure, who has knowledge of their fate." He cast about but there was no one left to ask. The crowds had long since fled back to their farms and villages, the performing animals temporarily corralled further down river away from the stench of smoke. The once vibrant community had been reduced to ash.

"What did he mean?" asked Thomas as he stuffed the enchanter's potion jar beneath his jerkin. "Who is the phoenix?"

Miles frowned. "Maleficius talks in riddles. Ignore him. The boy is a blind urchin, nothing more, but he pulls in the crowds and Maleficius will miss his purse. He uses us to locate the child that is all."

"Do not discount his words, Miles," Jesmina panted as she picked up her skirts and quickened her pace, "Maleficius speaks..."

"Jesmina, for pity's sake - enough!" Miles rounded on her, his palms raised, his patience exhausted. "I am weary of your support of the man. I care not what he says, or what you believe of him. The man is a fraud and a trickster. He serves only himself and if you are foolish enough to be deceived by his subterfuge, then I trust you will remain happy in your delusion."

"Miles." Thomas stepped forward to intervene on Jesmina's behalf but she held him at bay with a pointed look.

"You wish to find Edmund?" she countered sharply.

"That is my only wish."

"Then listen, knight, and you may find that the enchanter speaks a good deal more sense than you! You train your squire in your image do you not? To be true and honourable, to protect the weak and to withstand those who threaten."

Miles nodded.

"The boy Azim and Edmund are the best of friends, are they not?"

"Yes."

"Is it not likely then, that Edmund would seek to protect his young friend from a danger the child could not see and lead him to safety through the worst of the flames?"

Miles thought of Edmund, the bullied and beaten child who had blossomed in his care. Jesmina was correct, he was brave and true, and loyal to the point of madness, but he was also a mere child himself. The terror of the inferno had reduced grown men to hysteria. He found it difficult to believe that the lad would put himself in further danger voluntarily. Nevertheless it was possible that the two boys had sought shelter together. "Find one and we find the other, is that what you're saying?"

"That is what Maleficius was saying, but as usual you were too stubborn to listen."

Thomas grunted his agreement and Miles shot him a dark look.

"The feathered boy was in the barrel when last I saw him." Miles scanned the charred encampment, eyes narrowed as he assessed the carnage, and finally he spotted the wooden vessel, upturned and broken, its shattered remnants wedged against the lion's enclosure. "The barrel was emptied of water in the fight to vanquish the flames."

"Then the boy must have climbed out before the fire started," said Thomas.

"Perhaps he joined Edmund with the beasts. He was smitten with Edmund's dear little monkey." Jesmina's face creased with uncertainty as the fate of the monkey served as a grim reminder of what could have happened to the boys. She reached for Miles, and when he flinched from her touch her eyes drifted to the scorched flesh. "Your arm, Miles, you are injured...you must let me attend to it."

"You say all the horses were taken?" Miles brushed away Jesmina's concern and addressed the question to Thomas.

"Not all. Your destrier is missing, as is Edmund's mount. The miniature ponies were scattered about the place as if they had freed themselves and had no purpose. They are being gathered as we speak."

"What of your horse, Jesmina?" His warhorse, Coquet, and the stallion were the only beasts of real worth, if they were both missing then perhaps the intruders had been after horseflesh, not heretics, Templars, or strangely gifted children and the fire was simply an unhappy coincidence.

"I asked Edmund to tether him further downstream. The noise this evening unsettled him. I've checked and he remains quite safe."

Miles frowned. "Then I must borrow him from you, my lady, for it seems likely that wherever Coquet has gone, Edmund has followed. I did entrust the horse's safety to the lad, in fact I berated him for being tardy in his duties.

Jesmina slipped her hand in his once more and squeezed gently. "Do not blame yourself, Miles. You could not have predicted such an outcome. No one could."

"No one? The enchanter's wagon was unmarked while all around burned. How do you explain that?"

"I cannot explain it, Miles, but is Azim not also the property of Maleficius, precious property by all accounts? If the enchanter sought to protect his own would he not also ensure the safety of his boy?"

"As you were so quick to point out, Jesmina, and if Maleficius is correct, where we find one boy we will find the other. Perhaps he is more skilled in the dark arts than we imagine and protects his *familiar* from afar."

The horses were quickly saddled. The madness in the air had affected the stallion's sensibilities and it fought the bit in an attempt to take control. Miles was not unduly alarmed, he was more than a little exhilarated at the prospect of finally riding the animal he had coveted since Acre.

"I must accompany you," Jesmina pleaded, "Sultan obeys only one rider."

Miles shook his head. "Sultan will do as he is bid, Jesmina. Speed is of the essence, Thomas and I must ride swiftly if we are to catch up to the hooded ones. You would only add extra weight and work to the stallion's load and alas we can spare neither."

"Extra weight!" She huffed her indignation, hands on hips, pout on lips.

179

Miles turned his head to hide his amusement. "Think of the boy's, Jesmina."

"But..." she struggled for a plausible argument, "Your wound, I must accompany you, to tend to the wound. I am skilled in these matters as you know."

Miles stepped up into the saddle and the stallion danced beneath him. It skittered back and forth, nudging Thomas' heavier destrier aside. He took a moment to calm it with a few low words.

"The wound is nothing. I have suffered far worse. If need be I shall swallow my pride and use the enchanter's pungent potion. Believe me, you are more valuable here, Jesmina. The boys may yet appear, returned from an adventure unconnected to the mayhem. They will require your intervention to cushion them from the cruel snarl of the enchanter. I do not trust the man."

"Miles, we must make haste," urged Thomas. "The intruders have stolen a good few leagues upon us and we can only hope to shorten the distance under cover of darkness. If they have stolen your destrier and Edmund follows on his pony, with hopes of a rescue, then we must ensure that our little knight does not fall victim to his own recklessness. You of all people know the results of such unplanned acts." He glanced up at the cloudless sky. "We have a full moon to guide us, let us not waste it."

Reaching down from the saddle Miles cupped Jesmina's chin. Leaning further he pressed a fleeting kiss against her cheek. "Worry not, Jesmina, we shall return. I will not leave you at the mercy of Maleficius' whims. Whether you recognise the threat or not, Hugh would not wish it and I certainly do not."

Jesmina smiled tightly as if she doubted his words and believed it was the last she would see of him.

"Do you worry for my safety, Jesmina?" Miles teased as he fought to restrain the stallion.

"Pah!" she snorted in response. The hooded ones can take your hide and do their worst. Just be sure to return my stallion."

Seven

The moonlight guided them through rough terrain, the horses thundering on past the point where common sense would have indicated a rest or at the very least a slackening of pace. Once Thomas called out to Miles in a bid to slow them down, but Miles was deaf to all behind him. His mind was otherwise engaged trying to unravel the recent events. If simple horse thieves were the culprits then they would be dealt with accordingly and Miles looked forward to meting out their punishment. However, if Guy-de-Marchant were responsible for the unrest at the enchanter's encampment then it was unlikely Miles' favoured destrier, Coquet, was Guy's ultimate target. Guy's predilection for cruelty was renowned. Miles could not bear the thought of what he might do to Edmund or indeed Azim in retaliation for his humiliation in Acre.

"Miles, slow down for pity's sake." Thomas nudged his horse level and made one last attempt to broker common sense. "Jesmina's stallion might be game for this merciless dash, but my own mount is struggling. Slow down so that we may both reach our destination in one piece, or else I fear you will be tackling the rabble-rousers alone."

Faced with the prospect of losing his fellow knight by the roadside, Miles reined in the stallion and both men and horses took a well needed breather. "We are close, I feel it in here." Miles patted his chest with a gloved hand."

"All the more reason to be prepared, we do no good charging in. After all we are only two, against a count of

182

four at the least. There may be more, a whole body of men just waiting for their cohorts return. If Edmund and the enchanter's child are held captive, then we must plan the rescue well."

"You really believe Guy is involved in this?" Miles asked.

"I know he seeks you. He has made it known that he will pay handsomely for an opportunity to see you fall. The fact that your horse has been taken could be significant or merely coincidental."

"You think he may have paid men to draw me into a trap?"

"Possibly, it is just the kind of underhanded trick that Marchant is fond of. But there is more at play here, the fire, the missing child Azim. Maleficius seems overly concerned about his protégé. It would appear the enchanter has many enemies of his own and The Church has stoked their fears into a boiling pot. They see devilment in every shadow, who knows what they see when they look upon the enchanter's child. Is he so uncommon as to incite fear and hatred?"

"He is a child, Thomas. Strange and possessing of gifts others might covet - or fear, but a child nonetheless."

"And you, what do you think when you look at him?"

Miles shrugged. "I think nothing. As I say, he is a child, but half the size of Edmund. He dons a costume of feathers and runs the rope like he was born to do just that. Yet..."

"Yet what?"

Miles paused as he searched for an explanation of the disquiet he felt inside. "The boy...he...he is set aflame and yet he does not burn. He falls and yet he does not hit the ground. He is a trick of the light or sleight of hand, I do not know, it is beyond my understanding. I just wonder at Maleficius' words."

"That the child sees your destiny?"

"Yes. Maleficius has an uncanny knowledge of my circumstances. I puzzle at his source."

"He taunts you, Miles. He sees your weakness and he pokes at it with a well aimed stick."

"Perhaps. Nevertheless he is armed with more than a stick. You and I both know the damage that could be done if word of our exploits in Lincoln were to reach certain ears."

Thomas sighed. "I fear you obsess over an unlikely event. Our secret is safe. All parties held by oath under pain of death. You worry for naught. Let it be, Miles. In any event if the lad, this burning boy who commands such interest, could foresee the future, he would surely have foreseen this event and avoided his own capture."

Miles' lips twitched. "I'm not entirely sure the prophetic arts are quite so accommodating."

"What would I know, I have not travelled the past few months in the company of those who peddle such notions, but if it is true that the child sees beyond the end of this day, would you want to know what lies ahead?"

Miles wasn't sure. Did he wish to know the outcome of their current venture, the fate of his nemesis Marchant, or the name of his true love? A man could go mad just thinking of the possibilities. "I expect that would depend on whether I am to be blessed with a long and fruitful life."

"And if you were to die by the sword tomorrow?"

Miles grinned, "Then I would regret bestowing only one kiss on the lovely Jesmina."

They caught up with their quarry just as dawn was breaking. Weary from the journey, but exhilarated at the prospect of combat, they dismounted and refreshed themselves as best they could with water from a shallow stream. Thomas checked his crossbow and ignored Miles' frown.

"You intend to use that?"

"If I must."

"There is no skill in such a weapon," Miles declared. "They are knight-killers of the worst kind. We have both witnessed it."

"Aye, we have indeed." Thomas' hand strayed to his shoulder where he carried the ragged scars of a bolt. Only Hugh's skill had saved his arm."

"An arrow must follow a true line to hit its mark. A sword must be wielded with great strength and courage, but the bolt from such a contraption can be fired by any man-at-arms and still kill a king."

Thomas shrugged his response. "I do not wish to kill a king, merely a man without honour."

Miles reached out and took the heavy bow, weighing it carefully between both hands. It was indeed a fearsome weapon. He aimed it at Thomas and smiled. "Guy? Nay, he is mine. You shall not catch him with a bolt."

Leaving their mounts to drink their fill they made their way carefully to a secure vantage point.

Two men sat close to the remains of a campfire in the shadow of a rocky escarpment. One attempted to rekindle the flames and encourage the cooking of a freshly caught fowl, while the other pulled his cloak more snugly around his shoulders and muttered at the heavy dew that coated everything. There was a hint of frost in the shadows where the sun's rays had not yet reached, and no doubt when the sun had risen fully it would chase away the chill, but for now Miles and Thomas shared the man's ill humour. The heat of the hearth beckoned as they scanned the area from a meagre collection of stunted trees and shrubby undergrowth.

"We need to get closer," muttered Miles.

"Hold fast," cautioned Thomas. "Let us get the measure of our prey before we risk life and limb. They are only two, an easy victory it seems, but where are their comrades? Do they lie in wait? They may not even have the boys we seek. Let's not engage in unnecessary combat, where discourse might prevail."

185

Miles shot Thomas a sideways glance. "My friend, you sound more like Hugh every day."

"I merely suggest caution."

Miles pointed to an area beyond the camp where a line of horses were tethered. "They have my destrier and Edmund's pony and that is enough for me." He made to rise and was yanked back down by Thomas.

"Look, visitors."

Miles focused on the two riders who entered the camp on sturdy mounts. It seemed they too had ridden through the night, but by a more direct route, for they appeared unhurried and unruffled by the journey. Although their faces were obscured by distance, Miles had seen the men before and knew that despite sharing similar characteristics to the Mongol warriors he had fought in The Holy Land, they hailed from further afield. They had an aura of aloofness that suggested high status and after taking a moment to survey the small campsite they greeted the hooded ones with a curt dip of the head before dismounting. One of the dissenters rushed to take their mounts. His manner suggested a wary respect for the new arrivals which was at odds with the earlier loutish behaviour.

"What do you make of that?" asked Thomas. "Your rabble-rousers are struck dumb by the sight of a silken robe. Perhaps they imagine the exotic wrappings contain female flesh."

Miles snorted. "They will be sorely disappointed. The Orientals are the very same who were closeted with Maleficius prior to the fire. I can attest to the fact that they are indeed men, though Jesmina might make light of that assessment. Do not be fooled by their colourful trappings or courtly manners. I fear a plot far more complicated than we envisaged."

"A coincidence indeed," remarked Thomas. They seek counsel with the enchanter and before the day is out, his

186

cavalcade is naught but ashes and his *familiar* has disappeared."

"And now it appears they are about to break bread with the hooded ones."

"Break bread..." Thomas groaned.

Miles risked a quick smile. "Your belly must wait a while longer, friend. Once we have dealt with these wrong-doers, you may take your fill of whatever cooks over their fire."

"I shall die of hunger before a sword is drawn."

"Be strong, Thomas. I smell roasted fowl. What better incentive to wield a blade."

"A pre-arranged meeting, the Orientals were expected," remarked Thomas. "No raised weapons."

"No friendly welcome either. I suspect that we witness a business transaction and by the subservient manner of the ruffians, I imagine the Orientals have the upper hand."

"A trade? I doubt they have need for a destrier," said Thomas.

"Then what, the magician's pet?"

"Not merely a pet, Miles, a seer, according to Maleficius. You said it yourself, the child is uncommon. Who can measure the value of such a commodity?"

"Treasure indeed." Miles murmured as he recalled Maleficius' words and tried to unravel their meaning. When he could not, he returned his attention to the men in the camp. Their interaction appeared stilted as if the Orientals were dissatisfied with their initial discourse and the men who greeted them were unable to rectify the situation. When the sound of an approaching horse drew the attention of those in the camp, the men relaxed and it became clear that the transaction was to be handled by another, more able, negotiator.

Miles leaned forward as his enemy came into view. "Marchant! The murdering son of a poisoned sow is at the root of this evil just as you suggested." His impulsive reaction to reach for a weapon was quelled by Thomas' warning hiss.

"Wait." Thomas gripped him firmly. Without the older knight's caution Miles accepted he would have blundered in without concern for his own safety or the consequences. Instead, he took heed of Thomas' warning and watched with some impatience as Guy dismounted and, with his customary swagger, approached the eastern traders.

"Can you see Edmund or Azim?" Miles wriggled closer, taking temporary cover behind a rough screen of rocks. Thomas scanned the campsite and shook his head.

"They may be held elsewhere, we must hold fast. If Guy intends to trade the boys he must produce them sooner or later."

"We must act now," muttered Miles. We do no good here. If we cannot intervene then we must at least hear what is being said."

Moving with caution across the rough terrain, the two men closed the distance until a mere twenty paces separated them from the object of their scrutiny. To Miles' increasing concern, despite the close quarters there was still no sign of the missing boys.

Eight

The spokesman tipped his head with courteous regard, but the attempt at good grace was wasted on Guy whose mouth twisted into a contemptuous smirk. "We had an agreement," the man stated.

"An agreement? Sir, I have the item you desire. It falls to you to offer a suitable trade."

The Orientals muttered to one another, their language as exotic as their garb, heads bowed as they considered this response. At length the spokesman replied, "The trade is already made. You requested that the enchanter's camp be destroyed, that it should appear to be at his own hand. This we have done. A fiery hell has consumed everything in its path. Evil begets evil and the righteous bow their heads in prayer."

"*Everything* is destroyed?"

"The flames show no mercy, they consume the trappings of man with the same fervour as a drought parched beast slakes his thirst at the first fall of rain."

"And what of those who travelled with him?" Guy leaned in, eager for the detail. His eyes alight with fascination as if he regretted not being witness to the horror for himself.

"The misfits and the malcontent? The performing beasts and oddities?"

"Everyone," replied Guy, "Every last aberration."

"We simply prepared and positioned the powders. Your men were responsible for the ignition. If they followed your command no creature, man nor beast, could survive. The heat of such a firestorm would not allow it. The enchanter's collection of disordered fools had not the wit for defence against such catastrophe. You may rest assured they are all dead. Maleficius is a fool. He refused our barter for the child, we accepted yours instead. The enchanter alone must bear the consequences."

Guy turned to his men for confirmation. "And you, did you see this with your own eyes? Can you confirm this to be true?" The men shifted nervously.

"We know of only two survivors, my lord, and we have them here as you instructed."

"Plucked from the inferno, at great risk to ourselves," boasted the cockier of the two.

From their place of concealment Thomas shot Miles an encouraging glance and he returned it with a nod. His revulsion at the wicked plot was overshadowed by relief. Perhaps in carrying out Guy's orders to kidnap the boys, the men had ultimately saved their lives.

Guy grinned slyly, obviously more satisfied with the word of his own men, then that of the Orientals. "So it would seem that my enemy the upstart Miles of Wildewood has perished. How unfortunate that I am denied the final blow. I must make haste to the king and ensure his advisor Hugh-de-Reynard is notified of his protégés demise." He affected a dramatic sigh. "Ah, it pains me to be the bearer of such bad news."

"You are satisfied with our part of the bargain?" The trader eyed Guy with renewed interest, intrigued perhaps by his obvious delight at the loss of life.

"Satisfied? Oh yes. I am content with the outcome."

"Then we respectfully request that you settle payment. We have an arduous journey ahead and seek to begin it at the earliest opportunity."

Guy shrugged. "As you wish." He nodded to the men who hovered near the fire and they left the heat of the hearth and slipped between the tethered horses, pushing aside those that were slow to move, to reveal a place of concealment hewn from the rock escarpment.

"So the man plots my demise," muttered Miles to Thomas. "He does not know me well enough if he thinks I am so easily extinguished. Now, while the men-at-arms are otherwise engaged we must make our move. I look forward with relish to Guy's surprise when he sees me back from the dead."

"Patience, Miles," Let us be sure they have what we seek before we engage in hostilities. You saw four dissenters at Maleficius' encampment, there are still two unaccounted for. They could be lying in wait."

"They do not expect us, Thomas. Guy believes me dead. He believes us all dead, Maleficius included...and he will live to regret that error. It gives us an uncanny advantage"

"He believes what he has been told. His men tell him what he wants to hear, they do not know the truth of it for they fled before the flames were fully formed. The Orientals are a different story. I believe they play a different game. I begin to think Maleficius is an innocent party in all of this."

"Innocent, Pah! The man exudes guilt in every fibre. He exhales it with every rancid breath and pisses his poison daily against the wall. If he has not specifically plotted this deed then his darkness will have him complicit in some way. All the more reason for us to make a move, now, before the plotters are alerted to each other's subterfuge."

Thomas reached out and gripped Miles' arm firmly. "Wait," he implored.

Pain caused Miles to curse as Thomas' fingers tightened on the scorched flesh of his forearm. "Dear Lord, it is naught but a scratch, Thomas, yet it burns like the hottest oil. Marchant would have me burned alive along with Maleficius and his followers. Imagine the pain of that. A noble death in battle, by sword or axe or archer's arrow is one thing. But to be burned as a heretic, that is not a prospect I wish to think upon. What kind of a man draws pleasure from such wickedness?"

"A black-hearted knight, but then you have always known him as such. Here, try the enchanter's potion and prove to me that he is the trickster you believe. It will either soothe the fire and prove you wrong, or give you just cause to expose his devilment."

Miles snorted, "Fair enough, I will test the potion, but if my arm should shrivel and die before our eyes I'll hold you, not the enchanter, responsible."

Thomas grinned as Miles layered the noxious mixture onto the wound. "If the smell is equal to its power I suspect you shall be recovered by the time the sun is fully in the sky, but I pity your chances with any fair maiden, for they shall surely pull up their gowns and run a league at the stench."

"Just as I said, trickery," muttered Miles. "Maleficius' attempt to keep Jesmina's lustful eyes from straying my way, I tell you, the man is a devil indeed."

Thomas' laughter died on his lips as the attention of both men was drawn back to the camp by the return of Guy's men-at-arms. The first carried a sack over his shoulder. It hung to his waist, the weight sufficient that he used both hands to prevent it slipping from his grasp, but not so laden that he was caused to stoop. He placed it carefully on the ground in front of the Orientals and stepped back as if he expected a wild beast to spring from the sack and seek the nearest throat. Despite his caution, the load remained where he had placed it, unmoving. The second man dragged a squirming Edmund by the scruff of the neck. His hands were bound, the rope extending from his wrists to a loop around his neck, while the excess length was held securely in the soldier's hand. When the lad attempted a kick at his captor's ankles, he received a cuff to the ear for his troubles.

Miles lurched forward and again was restrained by Thomas. "How many times must I tell you...just wait."

The Orientals ignored Edmund's plight and observed the motionless sack for some moments. Despite their earlier claim to be keen to take their leave, they seemed almost reluctant to peer inside.

"The boy must be in the sack. They fear to gaze on the evil eye," said Thomas.

"They shall fear more than evil eyes if they attempt to take the child. Come, Thomas, we cannot delay. Guy intends some dark retribution for Edmund and the men from the East no doubt have plans for Azim. We can rescue both and put an end to Marchant's skulduggery if we act promptly.

"Does our treasure survive?" The question from the trader was directed at Guy, but for the answer, all eyes turned to the man who had carried the sack.

"He...he sleeps," stammered the man. He reached out with his boot and nudged the sack, but despite this additional prompt, the contents remained motionless.

"Do you suppose he has perished?" whispered Thomas. Miles shook his head. He found it hard to believe that having gone to the trouble of kidnapping this child to order, Guy's men would be remiss in his handling. If nothing else, the threat of Guy's displeasure would be enough to ensure the boy's survival. Miles watched as Guy switched his attention from the sack and circled Edmund slowly, head cocked as he assessed him.

"Edmund, it has been some time since we last met. How do you fare these past months? Does the bastard knight, Miles, care for you as he should?" His tone was at odds with his polite enquiry and Edmund flinched as if he expected a blow to follow. Guy tutted loudly, "Do you fear me, Edmund?"

Edmund shook his head defiantly, but his trembling lip and tear-filled eyes betrayed him.

Courage murmured Miles silently, though he wished that he could shout it aloud. *Have courage little man. We will not abandon you.*

"What a shame then that your protector has met with such an untimely end," continued Guy "and yet so fortunate that fate has delivered you back into my hands. I shall enjoy the re-acquaintance."

Miles reached for his sword. "If he lays a hand upon the boy's head, I shall gut him and leave the offal for the birds."

"Patience," warned Thomas, "this is not done yet."

"Our agreement?" reminded the Oriental trader brusquely. It appeared the men from the east did not share Guy's amusement at Edmund's disquiet. They exchanged sidelong glances as if they suspected some change of plan.

"Ah yes. You see, Edmund, these gentlemen are most anxious to see what the sack reveals. Shall they be disappointed? Does the feathered *familiar* merely sleep or have my men-at-arms been over zealous in their capture of your friend?"

Edmund's gaze slid with visible reluctance to the pathetic bundle. He drew a large breath.

"If he be dead, then ye shall all be cursed!"

The words spurted out from the child's mouth, high pitched and frantic, as though he had fought to contain them, and lost the battle. He closed his eyes tight, wincing in anticipation of Guy's response, a fist to the side of the head or a kick to his rear, but the man did neither.

"Cursed you say." Guy sniggered. The men-at-arms took another step away while the men from the east stepped closer. "Then perhaps you would do us the service of untying the rope that binds the sack and if any cursing is to be done, you may alert us to the prospect so we may take the necessary precautions. He crossed himself mockingly.

"Presumably Guy does not appreciate the value of the seer or he would not be so offhand regarding his welfare, or so quick to hand him over," murmured Miles.

Thomas gave him a sidelong glance. "He is not delivered yet. I suspect more trickery afoot. Guy is enjoying this performance too much. In any event I thought you did not believe in such tales of prophecy and forward sight."

Miles shrugged. "It is not I who wish to purchase such a boy. If I believed, then I would pay as high a price as demand dictates. The men from the east regard these wisdoms differently. Perhaps they wish to parade him through the streets or have him reveal the outcome of their next military campaign. Perhaps our own monarch would value such a pet, but our job is simply to return him to his rightful owner and retrieve Edmund in the process."

"The sack," prompted Guy. He made a great show of drawing his sword before jabbing Edmund to reiterate his command. The prod was no more than that, a show of power, a message aimed more at the Orientals than the boy, but all the same Miles simmered with pent up fury. He could not wait much longer to act, despite Thomas' entreaty.

Edmund opened first one eye and then the other. When it became evident that Guy's sword was not poised to pierce his heart, he crouched and began to fumble with the rope. It seemed the entire camp held its breath while he struggled to untie the knot while his own wrists remained tightly bound.

Despite Thomas' caution, Miles was determined Edmund should know that help was at hand. He pursed his lips and whistled softly, a gentle sound easily mistaken for the call of a bird, but one among them knew the call for something else entirely. Having heard the haunting sound many times before, Coquet's ears twitched in recognition. The mighty horse lifted his head and whinnied in response. Edmund raised hopeful eyes from the task at hand and watched the beast as it scanned the boundaries of the camp. In turn, the boy did the same. When his eyes fell upon his protector hidden within the shadows, Miles pre-empted any unwise reaction with a finger pressed to his lips. The lad dropped his gaze back to the sack lest his excitement be revealed to his captor.

"Hurry boy, we have no time for dawdling." Guy made a further show of swinging his sword. This time, in great sweeping motions as if he re-enacted a favourite battle. The sound of the sword as it cut the air was the only noise to break the expectant silence.

Edmund nodded and with a quick glance at Miles for reassurance he pulled open the sack and allowed the material to fall to the ground.

Inside, cross-legged at the bottom of the sack was the boy, Azim. His feathered costume was in disarray, the plumes ragged and limp. His ebony skin had lost its usual lustre and his eyes were closed, his breathing so shallow it appeared that he had indeed succumbed to the brutality of the previous hours. He was not the vibrant child who Miles recalled from the previous evening's show. Indeed he recognised the strange lacklustre posture as that displayed by Maleficius in the aftermath of the fire.

"Azim," whispered Edmund fearfully, "Azim, please wake. There are men here who wish to meet yer." He took the smaller boy's hand and squeezed it gently.

Guy took a step back, "Dear Lord above, what is that stench? Have we caught ourselves a polecat or a boy?" He raised a hand to cover his nose, while behind him, the Orientals began to mutter. The merchandise was patently not as they expected.

Miles and Thomas exchanged a glance.

"The enchanter's potion?" murmured Miles. He pulled back his sleeve and inspected his wound, raising it to his nose briefly to reacquaint himself with the pungent odour. The stench was concentrated, one inhalation enough to sour the nasal passages, but lingering just out of reach was a familiar undertone of opiate. Although the skin beneath the ointment remained angry and red, the pain was numbed. He glanced back at the boy, puzzled.

"What? What are you thinking?"

"I'm not certain, Thomas, though I believe I may have done Jesmina a disservice and Maleficius may yet prove me wrong." He scanned the campsite. "How many do you count?"

Thomas strained to see further. "The two Orientals, two hooded men and Guy. Five in all."

"What of the others? We are still missing two."

"There are only two tethered horses in addition to yours. Guy's mount is at his side, all the better for a quick retreat when he catches sight of my crossbow," he added with a quick grin, "and the men from the east surrendered their mounts to the men-at-arms when they arrived. The others must rendezvous elsewhere."

"Let's hope they do not seek reinforcements," said Miles. "We cannot hope to take more than five."

"The Orientals will not fight. I have met their kind before. They proffer peace when in truth they are a nation of plotters. They fight with words and false wisdom, but when faced with a sword they will back down."

"Are you certain of that, Thomas, I have met some fierce warrior monks, just look to our own for proof of that. If they have come this far for the uncommon child they may be prepared to fight for him."

"Then we must ensure we have the advantage."

Nine

Guy approached the feathered boy warily. "Is he entranced?" When Edmund's bewildered shrug provided no answer he turned back to the Orientals. "No matter. Our deal is done, gentlemen. Your boy delivered as agreed. Take him and be gone before we are all cursed with the devil's own stink." He motioned for his men to step away, to leave the strange child to his fate. "Break camp, we have a way to ride before we reach the king's entourage and I dearly long to see the Fox's face when he learns of his protégé's demise. That moment is best savoured in daylight, I think."

"One moment, sir," the Oriental raised a hand. "We must test the merchandise. He could be any urchin, pulled from alley or hovel. We require proof that he is The Burning Boy."

"You wish me to set him alight?" Guy's brow raised in surprise.

"It is the only way. Either he will burn or he will not."

As Guy reached for a length of burning firewood, Edmund threw himself in front of the child, looping his bound arms over the boy's head so he could clasp him tightly.

"Azim, please wake!" he pleaded.

"Move, boy or you shall burn along with the magician's spawn."

"I think not. No child will burn this day." Miles stepped out from the shadows and tossed a grim smile at Guy.

Thomas stood by his side crossbow raised and aimed. "Step away Guy, lest you be acquainted with the bite of a bolt. I do not recommend it."

"M...Miles?" Guy's confusion at the appearance of his enemy furrowed his brow. His grip on the burning branch tightened as did his grip on his sword. He flicked an accusing glance at the Orientals.

Miles moved closer. He could not resist a mocking smile. The sight of Guy left speechless was one to savour. "I fear your agreement with these eastern, potion pedlars is flawed. You place your trust in men you do not understand. Alas they have deceived you. As you can see I am very much alive, as are the followers of the great enchanter Maleficius. You plot with men far more skilled in the dark arts than you can possibly imagine, is it any wonder that they trick you and mock you."

"That is untrue, sir." The Oriental glowered at Miles, while behind him, his cohort mumbled discontent. He turned his anger back at Guy, his voice rising along with his ire. "Your own men fail you. See how they avoid your gaze and squirm with guilt. If they do not follow your orders, the blame for this error must rest on your shoulders not mine." The man shifted his attention to the two huddled boys. "I demand payment as agreed."

"Payment - payment! I shall give you payment." Guy spun on the balls of his feet. He dropping the lighted branch and swung his sword in the same motion. "Take it with my pleasure." The blade, honed to perfection, sliced through the Oriental's throat and the man's head snapped back. He was dead before he hit the ground. His eyes wide open, an expression of shocked disbelief frozen on his face. As the fallen man's blood puddled out from under him, his cohort turned and fled, silken robes flapping wildly as he ran. "After him," yelled Guy.

Edmund howled his terror as the discarded burning branch ignited the sacking beneath the feathered boy and he found himself trapped by his own courageous act. He struggled to pull Azim free, but tangled as he was within his own constraints; his efforts simply brought them closer to the flames.

The men-at-arms dithered, their fear of Guy's retribution eroding what little loyalty they possessed. Thomas settled their indecision by slamming a well aimed bolt into the chest of the nearest. As he footed the crossbow to re-load, the remaining soldier dropped the end of Edmund's rope and ran for his horse.

"Get back here," yelled Guy, but the man did not respond and in desperation Guy snatched up the trailing rope and held it taut. One sharp tug dragged both boys nearer to the flame.

Miles, skidded to a halt feet from Guy. His sword was raised, but he held it steady. The flames caught the fibres of the sack and it suddenly became clear that the same substance the Orientals had scattered at will around the enchanter's camp, had impregnated the material and it began to flare alarmingly. Edmund whimpered and Guy began to laugh.

"Who has the upper hand now, Miles?"

"Drop the rope and release the boys or suffer the consequences. I shall think naught of finishing what was started in Acre. In fact I relish the opportunity."

"You delude yourself, Miles. I would not sully myself with hand-to-hand combat with a bastard pretender. Back away now."

"To what purpose? You cannot defeat us both, Guy. Your man has run with his tail between his legs. My brother-in-arms has a bolt trained at your head. Fight me alone and you have the opportunity to recover your dignity. I will ensure that your family learns of your glorious death in battle. Surely you would rather that, than they suffer the shame of your dishonour?"

"Miles!" Thomas' urgent tone drew Miles attention and he flicked a glance at the boys. As Edmund tried to edge away, Guy simply yanked him back. Miles sought wildly for a solution.

"You miscalculate your position, Miles. My man does not run from you, or me, he runs for reinforcements. Do you imagine I ride alone in this Godforsaken place? My soldiers are moments away, twelve strong and starved of killing. I fancy you will burn along with your squire after all. Such a shame that those obsessed with the burning boy shall not see him ignited. It is a fearsome sight so I am told...isn't that correct, Miles?"

The flames grew stronger, purple fingers stretching out to ensnare tender young flesh. Edmund drew up his feet and wrapped his arms more tightly around Azim's small frame.

"Hold fast, Edmund. You are brave beyond measure. And you are almost saved," called Miles.

"Almost..." the despair in Edmund's response twisted deep in Miles' gut. He tightened his fist around the hilt of his sword and pain shot up his arm. *Pain?* Miles glanced at his arm; the lotion had been all but rubbed clear by his sleeve. *Treasure – Maleficius' treasure.* He smiled, his expectation of a favourable outcome increased immeasurably.

"Thomas, would you be so kind as to bestow the enchanter's gift on our young friend."

"Huh?"

"The potion! For pity's sake throw the jar."

Thomas frowned. He could not throw the jar without lowering his weapon.

Miles recognised his dilemma. "Trust me."

"Potions?" Guy sniggered. "You spend too long at the enchanter's side. Do you imagine magic will come to your aid?"

"No," replied Miles calmly. "I imagine knowledge will come to my aid.

Thomas lowered the weighty crossbow leaving Miles unprotected and threw the jar towards Edmund.

"Catch!" yelled Miles, but Edmund's attention was on the encroaching flames and the jar missed his outstretched hand and smashed at his feet, spraying its contents over both boys. As the potion touched Azim, his milky white eyes shot open. He reached out his small hands and began to scoop the contents applying the foulness to skin and feather. "No matter, Edmund" called Miles, "follow the boy's lead. The potion will protect you from the flames."

Guy dropped the rope and yelled his outrage at being outsmarted. With nothing to trade and no soldiers to protect him, he was left with no option but to fight. He raised his sword high above his head and brought it down towards Miles' head.

"Take care, Miles!" Thomas's warning came almost too late as Miles sidestepped and a glancing blow with the flat of the blade caught his shoulder. The edge of the blade would have taken his arm, nonetheless the weight of the blow sent him sprawling.

"See to the boys," yelled Miles as he rolled away from another blow and struggled back to his feet."

Thomas scrambled to the burning sack. The flames had been subdued by the noxious tincture. He stamped out those that remained and unravelled the rope that bound Edmund. Scooping Azim under one arm he took Edmund by the hand and ran them both to the safety of the tethered horses.

"Are you hurt?" he asked Edmund as he roughly checked the smaller boy for any sign of injury, lifting each skinny arm and patting down his tiny torso. Edmund shook his head and watched anxiously as if he expected Azim's entire body to be scorched. The feathered boy, miraculously unmarked by the flames, reached out a hand and Edmund grasped it tightly.

"We are safe, Azim," whispered Edmund. "I told yer me master, Miles would save us."

Thomas hefted Edmund onto Coquet's broad back and placed Azim in front; ensuring Edmund had tight hold of both child and reins. "Be ready, Edmund. We are not safe yet. The bastard Guy has reinforcements on the way." He tied the pony's reins to the larger animal's saddle and pointed beyond the surrounding scrubland to where his own horse and Jesmina's stallion remained hidden. "Go now, head for the rocks and wait by our mounts. Coquet is sure footed, he will see you there safely and we will follow."

"What of Miles?" Edmund asked.

Thomas glanced back to where Guy and Miles squared up to one another. "It seems I must, once again, extricate him from an ill advised encounter."

"You dance like a harem whore," mocked Guy as he pressed his advantage and forced Miles to take a defensive step back.

"And you should know, Guy. Did your mother introduce you to her sisters?"

The blades clashed heavily as each man sought to best the other. Equally matched in size and strength the deciding factor would be the depth of their animosity. Miles was certain he would be the victor. He parried Guy's blows until the wound on his forearm protested and then, when he sensed his enemies stamina had begun to falter, he began his assault. Having been thwarted in all previous attempts to finish his nemesis he was determined to savour the moment.

"Do you tire, Guy? Does the sword grow heavy?"

Guy glowered, "You shall feel its weight when it pierces your heart, peasant."

Miles laughed, "You have not the strength or skill, Guy. You stumble and drool like a half-wit. Are you certain you are not better placed in Maleficius' troupe? He is short of a jester. I'd be happy to recommend you." He circled his enemy delivering blows to tire him further, just waiting for the opportunity when Guy would lower his guard.

"Miles!" Thomas' urgent shout barely registered, such was Miles' focus on his opponent. "Miles! Enough of this horseplay. Finish it or leave it for another occasion. I hear horses. Many horses. I fear unwelcome guests approach."

Miles faltered, distracted for a split second and the momentary lapse was all that Guy required in order to gain the advantage. He thrust his sword, a lucky swipe that lacked any great momentum but nonetheless was sufficient to cut a swathe through Miles' padded aketon, and slice his flesh. Its destructive journey only curtailed when steel was confronted by rib-cage. Miles buckled and Guy advanced for the kill.

Thomas hefted the crossbow and took aim but before he could release the bolt his focus was distracted by another. The remaining Oriental, assumed long gone, approached from behind Guy. He stepped over the body of his fallen comrade without pause but when he caught Thomas' eye the message in the cold glance was unmistakable - Vengeance.

From beneath his robes he produced a staff, gaily coloured and intricately carved. He raised it as a peasant would raise a scythe and just as Guy hefted his sword to deliver his fatal blow, the Oriental swung the staff at Guy's head and it connected with a sickening thud. The man crumpled like a felled beast.

As Thomas scrambled to Miles aid, the Oriental paused to assess the scene.

"Go quickly," prompted Thomas, "The soldiers are almost upon us." The man took the time to crouch at the spot where the sack had burned. With a thin smile he picked up the shards of broken jar and rubbed the remaining drops of potion between finger and thumb, as if the gesture alone would reveal the sense of what had just transpired. When the sound of the approaching horses grew louder, he cast aside the shards, mounted his own horse and departed.

"Miles, can you walk?"

Miles grunted as Thomas hauled him to his feet, "A flesh wound, nothing more. Is he dead?" He cast a backward glance to Guy's prone body, blood leached from his head wound.

"As good as. Come away Miles. You can do no more. We must make haste before the rest of his minions arrive and we are held to task for the Oriental's deed."

"The boys?"

"They are safe and unharmed. It appears the great and wondrous Maleficius protected them from afar after all."

Ten

It was not easy for Miles to admit that he was wrong. In fact in many respects he was unwilling to believe that he was. But in the matter of Maleficius and The Burning Boy it seemed self evident that the boy was held in much regard by the enchanter and not simply because of his skill.

The boy, once returned, was met with a greeting that could only be likened to that of a father reunited with a lost son. Miles wagered that this human side of Maleficius, hidden well beneath the guise of enchanter and heretic, would be a fleeting affectation, but it was there and it was genuine. Miles was strangely touched by it. Maleficius laid one gnarled hand on Azim's, shoulder, patting the boy as he would a favoured hound, while the boy sat contentedly at his feet, his fingers entwined in the enchanter's robe.

At length Maleficius withdrew his attention from the feathered child and studied the boy's rescuer instead. "You do me a great service, Miles of Wildewood. One I shall never forget. Someday I shall return the favour."

Miles glanced at Thomas. They were both anxious to be gone from the place. Miles had delayed their return to Hugh and the king for only as long as it took for Jesmina to ply her healing hands and for his wound to recover sufficiently to allow him to ride his horse and wield a sword. But he could not leave without knowing.

"Someday?" Miles looked to the child and recalled the enchanter's words regarding the boy's gift of foresight.

Maleficius acknowledged Thomas' warning frown with a twitch of his lips. "Miles, it seems your fellow knight worries that you seek knowledge that will damn you."

"Will I be damned? Is that what the future holds for me?"

The enchanter sighed. He shifted his gaze to Jesmina and acknowledged her with a smile of sorts. His disfigured mouth prevented anything that resembled an affectionate greeting but the intent was there.

I see you are dressed for a journey, Jesmina. Do you leave me?"

"She accompanies Thomas and I," Miles responded on Jesmina's behalf. "We answer Hugh's call. Jesmina has travelled with you long enough, Maleficius." Miles tensed, expecting some resistance, but it seemed the return of Azim had settled all debts and instead of argument Maleficius simply nodded his agreement.

"Send my regards to The Fox. I will no doubt see him again, in this life or the next." He rose to his feet, "Good travels one and all." He reached for another small jar and threw it to Thomas. "Here, I wager you will have need of this. Your young knight attracts darkness at every turn; here is something to cast it away."

Thomas turned the jar carefully in his hand. He resisted the temptation to open it. Instead he nodded his thanks and hurried Jesmina out of the wagon. They had bid their farewells. There was nothing further to say.

"Edmund, you displayed great courage in defending the boy. Azim wishes you to have a special gift."

Edmund stepped forward. Sadness filled his eyes as he crouched by his small friend. Azim raised his face and smiled. "For you my friend," he whispered and from his costume he plucked the longest feather. Jet black, yet in the candle light it seemed a myriad of colours danced from it for the boy's entertainment. Edmund gripped it tightly.

"Thank you," he mumbled before he turned and ran to join the others.

"Forgive him, Azim," said Miles. "He is sad to leave you behind." He turned back to the enchanter and lowered his voice. "The future?" he asked, "What does the boy see?"

Maleficius blew out a long breath and the child reached up and gripped his hand.

"Beware the tattooed man."

"Beware the tattooed man? What kind of prophecy is that?" replied Miles sceptically.

"One day you will meet such a man and deny him. He carries a message, heed it well. Deny him at your peril."

Miles turned away. Theatre - pure theatre. The man was just as he had first thought, a fraud and a trickster.

"And, Miles," continued Maleficius with a twisted smile.

"Yes."

"Your true love will lead you to adventures that even you cannot imagine."

"My true love?"

"There is only one. She awaits you on the other side."

"I told you not to ask," muttered Thomas. He gathered up his reins and pretended disinterest.

"What did he say?" asked Jesmina, "Tell us, we are agog with curiosity. Are you to be a great warrior, a rich man? Tell us, Miles. What does your future hold?"

Miles mounted Coquet carefully, giving due regard to his most recent wound. He shot a sideways glance at his travelling companions. Thomas, Jesmina and Edmund were all mounted and waited in varying degrees of expectancy for his response. The horses pranced and jostled at the promise of exercise. Their riders equally keen to begin their journey. Miles paused a moment to consider his answer. He doubted the truth of the enchanter's words but would heed them nevertheless.

"Well?" pressed Jesmina, her impatience unbound.

Miles grinned. "Maleficius consulted with the burning boy and revealed ...."

""Yes...what did he reveal, my lord?" Edmund's eyes were wide.

Thomas shook his head at the boy's excitement and Miles' grin broadened even more. "He revealed a most exciting and wondrous future, Edmund. He advised that my companions and I should prepare for many more adventures." He winked at Thomas. "So, my good friends, are we ready for the next one?"

*****

About the author

B.A. Morton writes historical romance, romantic suspense and psychological thrillers, from her home in Northumberland, England. She lives with her husband and a variety of animals in a listed cottage with a unique medieval history. She enjoys gardening, reading and the countryside.

Success in the international literary competition 'The Yeovil Prize' launched her career and her first crime novel, 'Mrs Jones'. A member of the Crime Writers Association, she currently has three novels and a novella published by Twisted Ink Publishing with further work planned in both the Wildewood series and the Tommy Connell Mystery series. 2015 will see an exciting new relationship with UK crime publisher Caffeine Nights.

Discover more about current and future projects at the following links.

http://bamorton.weebly.com/
https://www.facebook.com/TheWildewoodChronicles
https://www.facebook.com/TwistedInkPublishing

From the author

As a writer I seek inspiration from the world around me and the people and events within it. However, sometimes, the skeleton of a story lies far closer to home than you can imagine, as I discovered when I first began research for The Wildewood Chronicles.

The Wildewood Chronicles is the product of a vivid imagination, the love of a tall tale and a genuine interest in the history and folk lore of a remarkable area, Upper Coquetdale in Northumberland, England. Loosely based on the history of Harbottle (Ahlborett), its castle and medieval barons, the key names have been fictionalised, but the tale is interwoven around some interesting facts.

The chapel at Kirk Knowe, which is integral to the Wildewood plot, did exist, with mention of it from 11th to 14th century. Our current home is built upon its foundations. Local barons were baptised at the chapel and documentation suggests the existence of a crypt. During excavations in 1871 a skeleton was unearthed at the cottage and given its ecclesiastical past, I suspect there may be more within the site.

Our hero, Miles, is a work of fiction, as are his acquaintances and adventures. However, he could well have joined the 9th crusade and the king might well have rewarded his endeavours. Indeed the 'novellas' prequel series was borne of a need to shed light on Miles' experiences prior to his return to England

The domain of Wildewood is also fictitious yet located in an area of wild natural beauty that exists almost unchanged since medieval times. The ancient woods and the challenges of the terrain and elements are as real now, as then. Take a solitary walk through these woodlands or scale the rocky crags and I defy you not to feel the echoes of the past. The jingle of harness; the clash of sword and the creak of a taut bow can all be heard, if you listen carefully and with an open mind. Look long enough at the shadows and you too will wonder at the shifting shapes.

Northumberland, *the land of castles* is full of history just waiting to reveal itself. All you need is a little imagination.

Please enjoy a complimentary sample from 'Wildewood Revenge' book one of 'The Wildewood Chronicles' and do look out for 'Assassins Curse' the next book in the prequel novella series.

And finally, if you've enjoyed my work, I'd love to hear about it. So please take a few moments to let me know, by leaving a short review on Amazon.

B.A. Morton

Wildewood Revenge

The Wildewood Chronicles
Book One

T he boy came silently. A wraithlike shadow slipping unseen between trees cloaked in frost. He stooped as hoary tendrils threatened to entwine him in their icy embrace, a slender bow held tightly in one hand while the other gripped a brindle terrier by the rough hair at its scruff. The dog remained alert. Ears pricked, its tail twitched with anticipation; the rasp of its breath the only sound to be heard in the silence of the winter forest.

The boy flicked a nervous glance around the tangle of waterlogged tree roots and eerie, stagnant pools. Afraid to proceed and unwilling to retreat, he rose slowly to his full height and peered at the body.

Slumped where it had fallen, it lay half submerged in the icy depths, one pale frozen hand outstretched, damp hair, obscuring the face. His heart lurched at the reality of what had transpired. Summoning what little courage remained he made a hurried sign of the cross and backed carefully away.

Small and undernourished, with ragged, dark hair and clothes the colour of the forest, it was little wonder he'd remained unseen long enough to carry out such a heinous act. He paused, drawing on the strength of his natural camouflage and silently chanted the charms of protection he'd learned at the breast. The beat of his heart stilled and he stepped back through the thorny barrier of frozen bramble runners and drew close again.

He saw the blood first, staining the melt water as it seeped from the body, trapped within the confines of the frigid pool. He watched transfixed as the slickness spread and the body slid further beneath the blackness. He felt fear, an overwhelming sense of dread that welled unbidden from the centre of his being, despite the charms. Reaching out with a hesitant hand he paused midway and drew back quickly, as if scalded by some unseen source. The dog whined and the boy cocked his head, alert to whatever sound distracted it. Then he was up and running, back into the dense woods from whence he had come.

Light-footed, he covered the flooded ground easily. He dodged low branches and fallen trees with not a single snapped twig to shatter the silence, until, with relief as keen as a long held breath, he burst into the makeshift camp like a wild thing freed from a trap, and the phantoms he believed snapped at his heels were let loose. The horses strained at their tethers, whinnies of alarm accompanying the wild kicking at the anticipated threat. The roosting birds of the forest rose as one, a cacophony of alarmed pheasants and pigeons squawked and flapped for cover. Their noise reverberated around the small clearing and contributed to the overall commotion. The boy tripped, scattering embers from the smouldering fire, then recovered and steadied himself with an outstretched hand.

His stunned companion lurched backwards away from the shower of sparks, spilled the contents of his cup and muttered a curse beneath his breath as the hot liquid seared the back of his hand. He staggered awkwardly to his feet, dropped the cup in the dirt and stopped the lad's flight by grasping him firmly by the shoulders.

"For pity's sake, Edmund," he growled, flicking a wary glance around the camp. "What in God's name is wrong with you? You'll awaken the Devil himself with that racket."

"My lord, I've done a terrible thing," the boy gasped, glancing back over his shoulder fearfully. He took a ragged breath, his chest heaving with the effort. "I meant to take a deer, but I have taken a boy! I fear I've killed him."

The boy shuddered and the man felt the child's tremors through his own hands. The boy may be guilty of many things but he was not given to flights of fancy. Yet, there was no one in these woods. He would stake his life on it.

Miles of Wildewood - knight, mercenary and sometime scoundrel - possessed tracking skills that were second to none. He'd seen no signs when they'd made camp. He'd set up perimeter markers and traps, none of which had been tripped; he would have surely been alerted if they had. He chewed thoughtfully at his lower lip, narrowed his eyes and scanned the tree line. There was no movement, nothing amiss. Crossing to the tethered horses, he hushed them with a gentle hand and a soft mutter against velvet noses. Cocking his head, he paused and listened. The only sound to be heard was Edmund's frantic panting.

Turning back to the boy, he reached out a hand and shook him roughly. "Been at the ale again, eh, Edmund?" The boy was a devil for the drink.

"No, my lord, t'was a body, I swear it." There was no mistaking the terrified look on the boy's face. If there were any ale to be had, Miles reckoned the lad would have downed one there and then, just to quell the fear in his belly.

Miles cast an eye out to the gloom of the encroaching forest and sighed sourly. He had no urge to trample through water-logged mires. He was cold enough. He'd forgotten just how miserable a Northumbrian winter could be. His chest tightened with the effort of inhaling frigid air, but he couldn't afford to ignore the boy. If there was to be trouble then better he knew of it first-hand, rather than later at the hands of others. Pulling his knife from the leather sheath tied against his leg he turned back to the boy.

215

"Where, Edmund? Show me where this body lies."

Edmund led Miles swiftly back through the stillness of the forest, to the spot where his victim lay, allowing his master to see for the first time the limp and bedraggled body which had begun to slide of its own volition beneath the icy water of the woodland bog. The body was soaked and unnaturally still. Edmund's arrow expertly lodged in the thigh.

Miles paused to survey the scene, holding Edmund back with a raised palm. When he was satisfied that no one lurked in the shadows between the trees, he knelt on the sodden ground and with rough hands hauled the body clear of the water, noting with suspicion and mounting unease the rope tangled around the neck. He glanced up at the overhanging trees. He saw no limb that would have accommodated a makeshift gallows. What devilment had gone on here?

He removed the damp woollen hat and tossed it to the boy before smoothing the mud splattered hair back from the face and then leaning so close that his own warm breath would have tickled had the victim been conscious, he listened for sounds of breathing. He noted the pale smooth skin and fine bone structure, and was aware of a subtle fragrance, hovering just beneath the stink of rotting vegetation. He sat back on the damp ground pulling the body with him and assessed the situation.

"Edmund, you are indeed a fortunate miscreant. Despite your skill with the bow, your victim still lives." He grinned at the lad, who shook with relief. "But I see I need to further your education, for this is no boy. Don't you know a maiden when you see one?"

Although at a loss as to where this girl had come from, or how she'd breached his fail-safe systems, he had not the time to deliberate on the puzzle. He couldn't afford to linger, nor could he simply leave her to perish. In reality it would have been more convenient to pretend they'd not stumbled upon her and preferable for all concerned if

Edmund had not skewered her with his suspect aim.

But as a knight, reluctant or not, he had a code of sorts to uphold. He accepted that lately he had been more scoundrel than valiant defender of the crown. Circumstances beyond his control had seen his honour tested. Perhaps in the guise of this strange bedraggled girl, the fates had sent him a reminder of how he should behave. Who was he to argue with fate?

He loosened the noose from around the girl's neck, noting the redness of burnt skin, stripped off his belt and used it to stem the flow of blood. Then picking her up as if she weighed naught, he slung her across his shoulder as he would have carried the deer, had Edmund's aim had been true. With questionable care, and surprising speed he carried her back to the camp.

Dropping her limp body in an unceremonious heap by the fire, Miles pondered whether such a scrawny thing was worth his efforts at all. He had things to do. Plans that required set in motion, which he delayed at his own peril. There was no guarantee of her regaining her senses and, honour-be-damned, he'd no desire to be landed with a drooling halfwit. He crouched at her side, laid a palm against her cheek, and felt her skin cold and clammy. He knew her leg required treatment and the arrow must come out, but it was not safe to linger here in the frozen wood.

Whoever she was, her kin would come looking and he doubted they would believe young Edmund had mistaken her for a deer. They would either be looking to rescue her or finish her off, and waiting around to find out was not an option.

"What did you see before you loosed your arrow?" he asked the boy, impatiently. He needed to understand the significance of what they'd inadvertently stumbled upon. It was not usual to come across young girls, alone in the deep woods, even more unusual to discover them near death with a rope around their neck. Despite his impatience at this unwelcome interlude, he was intrigued.

217

Edmund shrugged, bewildered. "A deer, I reckon I seen a deer."

"But obviously you did not. Did you merely see movement? Was the girl on the ground or in the air?" He pictured her suddenly, a fleeting image of a terrified face, as she swung, feet far from the ground. His hand strayed to his throat, where his own scars were barely visible, but engrained on his mind nonetheless. He dropped his hand and blinked the image away.

"In the air," Edmund pulled a face, suppressing his laughter. "How could she be in the air, she's not a bird?" He flapped his arms, hopping on one leg, a court jester in the making. Miles recognised fear edging toward hysteria as the boy attempted to rationalise his actions. He recalled his own first kill. Fear mingled with elation. It had left a bitter taste, but that was long ago and his palate had quickly grown accustomed.

Continuing his assessment of the girl's condition, Miles ignored the boy's antics and his interest grew, despite his initial reluctance. In his experience everything happened for a reason, good or bad. It was his task to determine how best to turn this misadventure to his own advantage. "Nor is she a deer, Edmund, but that did not stop you. Was she hanging? Or was she on the ground?"

"Does it matter, my lord?" shrugged the boy in confusion.

"It matters if we have come upon a hanging," replied Miles grimly. "The hangman may come looking for his corpse." He turned with a menacing grin that highlighted the scar tracing his jaw line. He couldn't help himself. Edmund was such an easy target. "Or indeed, he may be content to take the boy who loosed the arrow, in place of the corpse. Just think of it, Edmund, the world looks quite different from the end of a rope." And he should know.

Edmund paused, one foot hovering above the ground and allowed his arms to drop to his side.

"I think she be on the ground," he said quickly. He'd no wish to meet the hangman.

Miles shook his head impatiently. "You think? Maybe if you had thought before you released the arrow we wouldn't be in this predicament." He didn't need the additional aggravation. Not now so close to home, so close to completing his mission.

"Edmund make haste, prepare the horses, we need to leave now." He snapped the shaft of the arrow, to ensure it did not impede their progress but the girl lay unresponsive to any additional pain the action may have caused. She was either made of sterner stuff than he, or so far gone the pain had ceased to mean anything.

He checked her breathing again. Detected it; shallow but still there. He slid a rough palm beneath the neck of her woollen jerkin, ignored the swell of her breasts and concentrated his mind on the rhythm of her heart beating in her chest. The physicians he'd met on his travels, in lands far from this place, had held great store by the function of the heart in life and death. He was no physician, but it was true, he'd never felt the beat within the chest of a dead man and he'd seen and created many dead men.

"Edmund did you hear me?" He withdrew his hand and turned impatiently. "What have you there?"

Edmund grinned mischievously, fear now erased from his face. He lifted the small dog by its scruff for inspection. "He's mine, I found him in yonder forest. He'll bring us many rabbits." The dog wriggled in the boy's grasp, wagged its tail energetically and Miles allowed a reluctant smile.

"Rabbits yes, but no more deer, Edmund, or the king will have your head and mine." The boy dropped his gaze and Miles momentarily shared his unease at the strange turn of events. He turned away from the child, swept a quick glance around the campsite and added gruffly. "Keep him if you must, but make sure he doesn't stray. He has a

219

wilful look about him. I fancy he would think naught of chasing my stock, supposing I have any left after all this time." The boy grinned again and nodded his agreement. "And, Edmund," added Miles, "make haste!"

Riding hard through the forest the horses picked their way sure-footedly through the bogs and beyond, where the moor rose above them, still snow covered. Here the land grew ever steeper and more rugged. The wind snapped cruelly across the vast empty terrain and the riders braced themselves against the biting weather.

All the while Miles held the girl against the warmth of his body. He fought the wheeze which tightened his chest as her cold impregnated him and he began to doubt his decision to bring her along. She would likely die and he would have received a soaking for naught.

Her head rested beneath his chin and he listened as she whimpered with pain. A good sign, she was regaining some of her faculties. He pondered on her identity, where she'd come from and how she'd gotten so close to them without being seen. He wondered about her strange clothes, and why she was dressed as a boy. Miles knew all about spies, had encountered more than a few on his travels. He knew how they worked, how devious they could be, but what would spies be doing this far north? Unless, word had got out of his return to these shores, and Sir Gerard had prepared a welcome.

He wondered a lot and in particular, he puzzled about why someone would want her dead. She was very young to warrant the noose, but who was he to question the law, or her, if indeed she had fallen foul of it. He had spent much of his time in questionable compliance with laws that changed as readily as the Monarch. It was not his place, nor his wish, to pass judgement on a scrap, who might yet succumb to her wounds.

His judgement was reserved for someone altogether more deserving.

Made in the USA
Charleston, SC
24 March 2015